Nicholson Baker

VINTAGE **BAKER**

Nicholson Baker was born in 1957 and attended the Eastman School of Music and Haverford College. He has published seven novels—*The Mezzanine* (1988), *Room Temperature* (1990), *Vox* (1992), *The Fermata* (1994), *The Everlasting Story of Nory* (1998), *A Box of Matches* (2003), and *Checkpoint* (2004)—and three works of nonfiction, *U and I* (1991), *The Size of Thoughts* (1996), and *Double Fold* (2001), which won a National Book Critics Circle Award.

VINTAGE BAKER

Nicholson Baker

VINTAGE BOOKS

A Division of Random House, Inc.

New York

A VINTAGE ORIGINAL, OCTOBER 2004

Copyright © 2004 by Nicholson Baker

All rights reserved under International and Pan-American
Copyright Conventions. Published in the United States by
Vintage Books, a division of Random House Inc., New York,
and simultaneously in Canada by Random House
of Canada Limited, Toronto.

Vintage and colophon are registered trademarks of Random House, Inc.

The pieces in this collection were published as follows:
Chapter One, Two, and Three from *The Mezzanine*, copyright © 1988
by Nicholson Baker. Used by permission of Grove/Atlantic, Inc.
The selection from *Vox*, copyright © 1993
by Nicholson Baker. The selection from *The Fermata*
copyright © 1994 by Nicholson Baker. "Rarity," "The Projector," "Reading Aloud,"
"Leading with the Grumper," and "Lumber" from *The Size of Thoughts* copyright © 1996
by Nicholson Baker. Chapter One and Two from *Double Fold*, © copyright 2001
by Nicholson Baker. Chapter Five, Six, Seven, and Eight from
A Box of Matches copyright © 2003 by Nicholson Baker.
Two illustrations appearing with "The Projector," copyright © 1994
by Mark Zingarelli. Used by permission of Mark Zingarelli.

Library of Congress Cataloging-in-Publication Data

Baker, Nicholson.
Vintage Baker / Nicholson Baker.
p.   cm
"A Vintage original"—T.p. verso.
ISBN 1-4000-7860-1
I. Title.
PS3552.A4325A6 2004
813'.54—dc22   2004052614

Book design by JoAnne Metsch

www.vintagebooks.com

Printed in the United States of America
10   9   8   7   6   5   4   3   2   1

CONTENTS

VINTAGE BAKER

Chapter One
from THE MEZZANINE

At almost one o'clock I entered the lobby of the building where I worked and turned toward the escalators, carrying a black Penguin paperback and a small white CVS bag, its receipt stapled over the top. The escalators rose toward the mezzanine, where my office was. They were the freestanding kind: a pair of integral signs swooping upward between the two floors they served without struts or piers to bear any intermediate weight. On sunny days like this one, a temporary, steeper escalator of daylight, formed by intersections of the lobby's towering volumes of marble and glass, met the real escalators just above their middle point, spreading into a needly area of shine where it fell against their brushed-steel side-panels, and adding long glossy highlights to each of the black rubber handrails which wavered slightly as the handrails slid on their tracks, like the radians of black luster that ride the undulating outer edge of an LP.[1]

---

[1] I love the constancy of shine on the edges of moving objects. Even propellers or desk fans will glint steadily in certain places in the grayness of their rotation;

When I drew close to the up escalator, I involuntarily transferred my paperback and CVS bag to my left hand, so that I
could take the handrail with my right, according to habit.
The bag made a little paper-rattling sound, and when I looked
down at it, I discovered that I was unable for a second to
remember what was inside, my recollection snagged on the
stapled receipt. But of course that was one of the principal
reasons you needed little bags, I thought: they kept your
purchases private, while signaling to the world that you led
a busy, rich life, full of pressing errands run. Earlier that
lunch hour, I had visited a Papa Gino's, a chain I rarely ate
at, to buy a half-pint of milk to go along with a cookie I had
bought unexpectedly from a failing franchise, attracted by
the notion of spending a few minutes in the plaza in front of
my building eating a dessert I should have outgrown and
reading my paperback. I paid for the carton of milk, and
then the girl (her name tag said "Donna") hesitated, sensing
that some component of the transaction was missing: she
said, "Do you want a straw?" I hesitated in turn—did I? My
interest in straws for drinking anything besides milkshakes
had fallen off some years before, probably peaking out the
year that all the major straw vendors switched from paper to
plastic straws, and we entered that uncomfortable era of the
floating straw;[1] although I did still like plastic elbow straws,

---

the curve of each fan blade picks up the light for an instant on its circuit and
then hands it off to its successor.

[1] I stared in disbelief the first time a straw rose up from my can of soda and
hung out over the table, barely arrested by burrs in the underside of the metal
opening. I was holding a slice of pizza in one hand, folded in a three-finger grip
so that it wouldn't flop and pour cheese-grease on the paper plate, and a paper-

back in a similar grip in the other hand—what was I supposed to do? The whole point of straws, I had thought, was that you did not have to set down the slice of pizza to suck a dose of Coke while reading a paperback. I soon found, as many have, that there was a way to drink no-handed with these new floating straws: you had to bend low to the table and grasp the almost horizontal straw with your lips, steering it back down into the can every time you wanted a sip, while straining your eyes to keep them trained on the line of the page you were reading. How could the straw engineers have made so elementary a mistake, designing a straw that weighed less than the sugar-water in which it was intended to stand? Madness! But later, when I gave the subject more thought, I decided that, though the straw engineers were probably blameworthy for failing to foresee the straw's buoyancy, the problem was more complex than I had first imagined. As I reconstruct that moment of history, circa 1970 or so, what happened was that the plastic material used in place of paper was in fact heavier than Coke—their equations were absolutely correct, the early manufacturing runs looked good, and though the water-to-plastic weight ratio was a little tight, they went ahead. What they had forgotten to take into account, perhaps, was that the bubbles of carbonation attach themselves to invisible asperities on the straw's surface, and are even possibly generated by turbulence at the leading edge of the straw as you plunge it in the drink; thus clad with bubbles, the once marginally heavier straw reascends until its remaining submerged surface area lacks the bubbles to lift it further. Though the earlier paper straw, with its spiral seam, was much rougher than plastic, and more likely to attract bubbles, it was porous: it soaked up a little of the Coke as a ballast and stayed put. All right—an oversight; why wasn't it corrected? A different recipe for the plastic, a thicker straw? Surely the huge buyers, the fast-food companies, wouldn't have tolerated straws beaching themselves in their restaurants for more than six months or so. They must have had whole departments dedicated to exacting concessions from Sweetheart and Marcal. But the fast-food places were adjusting to a novelty of their own at about the same time: they were putting slosh caps on every soft drink they served, to go *or* for the dining room, which cut down on spillage, and the slosh caps had a little cross in the middle, which had been the source of some unhappiness in the age of paper straws, because the cross was often so tight that the paper straw would crumple when you tried to push it through. The straw men at the fast-food corporations had had a choice: either we (a) make the crossed slits easier to pierce so that the paper straws aren't crumpled, or we (b) abandon paper outright, and make the slits even *tighter*, so that (1) any tendency to float is completely negated and (2) the seal between the straw and the crossed slits is so tight that almost no soda will well out, stain car seats and clothing, and cause frustration. And (b) was the ideal solution for them, even leaving aside the attractive price that the straw manufacturers were offering as they switched their plant

6 NICHOLSON BAKER

whose pleated necks resisted bending in a way that was very similar to the tiny seizeups your finger joints will undergo if you hold them in the same position for a while.[1]

So when Donna asked if I would like a straw to accompany my half-pint of milk, I smiled at her and said, "No thanks. But maybe I'd like a little bag." She said, "Oh! Sorry," and hurriedly reached under the counter for it, touchingly flustered, thinking she had goofed. She was quite new; you could tell by the way she opened the bag: three anemone splayings of her fingers inside it, the slowest way. I thanked her and left, and then I began to wonder: Why had I requested a bag to hold a simple half-pint of milk? It wasn't simply out of some abstract need for propriety, a wish to shield the nature of my purchase from the public eye—although this was often a powerful motive, and not to be ridiculed. Small mom and pop shopkeepers, who understood these things, instinctively shrouded whatever solo item you bought—a box

---

over from paper-spiraling equipment to high-speed extrusion machines—so they adopted it, not thinking that their decision had important consequences for all restaurants and pizza places (especially) that served cans of soda. Suddenly the paper-goods distributor was offering the small restaurants floating plastic straws and only floating plastic straws, and was saying that this was the way all the big chains were going; and the smaller sub shops did no independent testing using cans of soda instead of cups with crossed-slit slosh caps. In this way the quality of life, through nobody's fault, went down an eighth of a notch, until just last year, I think, when one day I noticed that a plastic straw, made of some subtler polymer, with a colored stripe in it, stood anchored to the bottom of my can!

[1]When I was little I had thought a fair amount about the finger-joint effect; I assumed that when you softly crunched over those temporary barriers you were leveling actual "cell walls" that the joint had built to define what it believed from your motionlessness was going to be the final, stable geography for that microscopic region.

of pasta shells, a quart of milk, a pan of Jiffy Pop, a loaf of bread—in a bag: food meant to be eaten indoors, they felt, should be seen only indoors. But even after ringing up things like cigarettes or ice cream bars, obviously meant for ambulatory consumption, they often prompted, "Little bag?" "Small bag?" "Little bag for that?" Bagging evidently was used to mark the exact point at which title to the ice cream bar passed to the buyer. When I was in high school I used to unsettle these proprietors, as they automatically reached for a bag for my quart of milk, by raising a palm and saying officiously, "I don't need a bag, thanks." I would leave holding the quart coolly in one hand, as if it were a big reference book I had to consult so often that it bored me.

Why had I intentionally snubbed their convention, when I had loved bags since I was very little and had learned how to refold the large thick ones from the supermarket by pulling the creases taut and then tapping along the infolding center of each side until the bag began to hunch forward on itself, as if wounded, until it lay flat again? I might have defended my snub at the time by saying something about unnecessary waste, landfills, etc. But the real reason was that by then I had become a steady consumer of magazines featuring color shots of naked women, which I bought for the most part not at the mom-and-pop stores but at the newer and more anonymous convenience stores, distributing my purchases among several in the area. And at these stores, the guy at the register would sometimes cruelly, mock-innocently warp the "Little bag?" convention by asking, "You need a bag for that?"—forcing me either to concede this need with a nod, or to be tough and say no and roll up the unbagged nude magazine and clamp it in my bicycle rack so that only the giveaway cigarette ad on the back cover showed—"Carlton Is Lowest."[1]

Hence the fact that I often said no to a bag for a quart of milk at the mom-and-pop store during that period was a way of demonstrating to anyone who might have been following my movement that at least at that moment, exiting that store, I had nothing to hide; that I did make typical, vice-free family purchases from time to time. And now I was asking for a little bag for my half-pint of milk from Donna in order, finally, to clean away the bewilderment I had caused those moms and pops, to submit happily to the convention, even to pass it on to someone who had not yet quite learned it at Papa Gino's.

But there was a simpler, less anthropological reason I had specifically asked Donna for the bag, a reason I hadn't quite

---

[1] For several years it was inconceivable to buy one of those periodicals when a girl was behind the counter; but once, boldly, I tried it—I looked directly at her mascara and asked for a *Penthouse*, even though I preferred the less pretentious *Oui* or *Club*, saying it so softly however that she heard "Powerhouse" and cheerfully pointed out the candy bar until I repeated the name. Breaking all eye contact, she placed the document on the counter between us—it was back when they still showed nipples on their covers—and rang it up along with the small container of Woolite I was buying to divert attention: she was embarrassed and brisk and possibly faintly excited, and she slipped the magazine in a bag without asking whether I "needed" one or not. That afternoon I expanded her brief embarrassment into a helpful vignette in which I became a steady once-a-week buyer of men's magazines from her, always on Tuesday morning, until my very ding-dong entrance into the 7-Eleven was charged with trembly confusion for both of us, and I began finding little handwritten notes placed in the most widespread pages of the magazine when I got home that said, "Hi!—the Cashier," and "Last night I posed sort of like this in front of my mirror in my room—the Cashier," and "Sometimes I look at these pictures and think of you looking at them—the Cashier." Turnover is always a problem at those stores, and she had quit the next time I went in.

isolated in that first moment of analysis on the sidewalk afterward, but which I now perceived, walking toward the escalator to the mezzanine and looking at the stapled CVS bag I had just transferred from one hand to the other. It seemed that I always liked to have one hand free when I was walking, even when I had several things to carry: I liked to be able to slap my hand fondly down on top of a green mailmen-only mailbox, or bounce my fist lightly against the steel support for the traffic lights, both because the pleasure of touching these cold, dusty surfaces with the springy muscle on the side of my palm was intrinsically good, and because I liked other people to see me as a guy in a tie yet carefree and casual enough to be doing what kids do when they drag a stick over the black uprights of a cast-iron fence. I especially liked doing one thing: I liked walking past a parking meter so close that it seemed as if my hand would slam into it, and at the last minute lifting my arm out just enough so that the meter passed underneath my armpit. All of these actions depended on a free hand; and at Papa Gino's I already was holding the Penguin paperback, the CVS bag, and the cookie bag. It might have been possible to hold the blocky shape of the half-pint of milk against the paperback, and the tops of the slim cookie bag and the CVS bag against the other side of the paperback, in order to keep one hand free, but my fingers would have had to maintain this awkward grasp, building cell walls in earnest, for several blocks until I got to my building. A bag for the milk allowed for a more graceful solution: I could scroll the tops of the cookie bag, the CVS bag, and the milk bag *as one* into my curled fingers, as if I were taking a small child on a walk. (A straw poking out of the top of the milk bag would have interfered with this scrolling—lucky I had refused it!) Then I could slide the paperback into the space between the scroll of bag paper and my palm. And this is what I had in fact done. At first the Papa Gino's bag was stiff, but very soon my walking softened the paper a little, although I never got it to the state of utter silence and flannel softness that a bag will attain when you carry it around all day, its handheld curl so finely wrinkled and formed to your fingers by the time you get home that you hesitate to unroll it.

It was only just now, near the base of the escalator, as I watched my left hand automatically take hold of the paperback and the CVS bag together, that I consolidated the tiny understanding I had almost had fifteen minutes before. Then it had not been tagged as knowledge to be held for later retrieval, and I would have forgotten it completely had it not been for the sight of the CVS bag, similar enough to the milk-carton bag to trigger vibratiuncles of comparison. Under microscopy, even insignificant perceptions like this one are almost always revealed to be more incremental than you later are tempted to present them as being. It would have been less cumbersome, in the account I am giving here of a specific lunch hour several years ago, to have pretended that the bag thought had come to me complete and "all at once" at the foot of the up escalator, but the truth was that it was only the latest in a fairly long sequence of partially forgotten, inarticulable experiences, finally now reaching a point that I paid attention to it for the first time.

In the stapled CVS bag was a pair of new shoelaces.

Chapter Two
from THE MEZZANINE

My left shoelace had snapped just before lunch. At some
earlier point in the morning, my left shoe had become untied,
and as I had sat at my desk working on a memo, my foot had
sensed its potential freedom and slipped out of the sauna of
black cordovan to soothe itself with rhythmic movements
over an area of wall-to-wall carpeting under my desk, which,
unlike the tamped-down areas of public traffic, was still almost
as soft and fibrous as it had been when first installed. Only
under the desks and in the little-used conference rooms was
the pile still plush enough to hold the beautiful Ms and Vs the
night crew left as strokes of their vacuum cleaners' wands
made swaths of dustless tufting lean in directions that alter-
nately absorbed and reflected the light. The nearly universal
carpeting of offices must have come about in my lifetime,
judging from black-and-white movies and Hopper paintings:
since the pervasion of carpeting, all you hear when people
walk by are their own noises—the flap of their raincoats, the
jingle of their change, the squeak of their shoes, the efficient
little sniffs they make to signal to us and to themselves that

they are busy and walking somewhere for a very good reason, as well as the almost sonic whoosh of receptionists' staggering and misguided perfumes, and the covert chokings and showings of tongues and placing of braceleted hands to windpipes that more tastefully scented secretaries exchange in their wake. One or two individuals in every office (Dave in mine), who have special pounding styles of walking, may still manage to get their footfalls heard; but in general now we all glide at work: a major improvement, as anyone knows who has visited those areas of offices that are still for various reasons linoleum-squared—cafeterias, mailrooms, computer rooms. Linoleum was bearable back when incandescent light was there to counteract it with a softening glow, but the combination of fluorescence and linoleum, which must have been widespread for several years as the two trends overlapped, is not good.

As I had worked, then, my foot had, without any sanction from my conscious will, slipped from the untied shoe and sought out the texture of the carpeting; although now, as I reconstruct the moment, I realize that a more specialized desire was at work as well: when you slide a socked foot over a carpeted surface, the fibers of sock and carpet mesh and lock, so that though you think you are enjoying the texture of the carpeting, you are really enjoying the slippage of the inner surface of the sock against the underside of your foot, something you normally get to experience only in the morning when you first pull the sock on.[1]

---

[1] When I pull a sock on, I no longer *pre-bunch*, that is, I don't gather the sock up into telescoped folds over my thumbs and then position the resultant donut

At a few minutes before twelve, I stopped working, threw out my earplugs and, more carefully, the remainder of my morning coffee—placing it upright within the converging spinnakers of the trash can liner on the base of the receptacle itself. I stapled a copy of a memo someone had cc:'d me on to a copy of an earlier memo I had written on the same subject, and wrote at the top to my manager, in my best casual scrawl, "Abe—should I keep hammering on these people or drop it?" I put the stapled papers in one of my Eldon trays, not sure whether I would forward them to Abelardo or not. Then I slipped my shoe back on by flipping it on its side, hooking it with my foot, and shaking it into place. I accomplished all this by foot-feel; and when I crouched forward, over the papers on my desk, to reach the untied shoelace, I experienced a faint surge of pride in being able to tie a shoe without looking at it. At that moment, Dave, Sue, and Steve, on their way to lunch, waved as they passed by my office. Right in the middle of tying a shoe as I was, I couldn't wave nonchalantly back, so I called out a startled, overhearty "Have a good one, guys!" They disappeared; I pulled the left shoelace tight, and *bingo,* it broke.

---

over my toes, even though I believed for some years that this was a clever trick, taught by admirable, fresh-faced kindergarten teachers, and that I revealed my laziness and my inability to plan ahead by instead holding the sock by the ankle rim and jamming my foot to its destination, working the ankle a few times to properly seat the heel. Why? The more elegant prebunching can leave in place any pieces of grit that have embedded themselves in your sole from the imperfectly swept floor you walked on to get from the shower to your room; while the cruder, more direct method, though it risks tearing an older sock, does detach this grit during the foot's downward passage, so that you seldom later feel irritating particles rolling around under your arch as you depart for the subway.

The curve of incredulousness and resignation I rode out at that moment was a kind caused in life by a certain class of events, disruptions of physical routines, such as:

(a) reaching a top step but thinking there is another step there, and stamping down on the landing;

(b) pulling on the red thread that is supposed to butterfly a Band-Aid and having it wrest free from the wrapper without tearing it;

(c) drawing a piece of Scotch tape from the roll that resides half sunk in its black, weighted Duesenberg of a dispenser, hearing the slightly descending whisper of adhesive-coated plastic detaching itself from the back of the tape to come (descending in pitch because the strip, while amplifying the sound, is also getting longer as you pull on it[1]), and then, just as you are intending to break the piece off over the metal serration, reaching the innermost end of the roll, so that the segment you have been pulling wafts unexpectedly free. Especially now, with the rise of Post-it notes, which have made the massive black tape-dispensers seem even more grandiose and Biedermeier and tragically defunct, you almost believe that you will never come to the end of a roll of tape; and when you do, there is a feeling, nearly, though very briefly, of shock and grief;

---

[1] When I was little I thought it was called Scotch tape because the word "scotch" imitated the descending screech of early cellophane tapes. As incandescence gave way before fluorescence in office lighting, Scotch tape, once yellowish-transparent, became bluish-transparent, as well as superbly quiet.

(d) attempting to staple a thick memo, and looking forward, as you begin to lean on the brontosaural head of the stapler arm,[1] to the three phases of the act—

first, before the stapler arm makes contact with the paper, the resistance of the spring that keeps the arm

---

[1]Staplers have followed, lagging by about ten years, the broad stylistic changes we have witnessed in train locomotives and phonograph tonearms, both of which they resemble. The oldest staplers are cast-ironic and upright, like coal-fired locomotives and Edison wax-cylinder players. Then, in mid-century, as locomotive manufacturers discovered the word "streamlined," and as tonearm designers housed the stylus in aerodynamic ribbed plastic hoods that looked like trains curving around a mountain, the people at Swingline and Bates tagged along, instinctively sensing that staplers were like locomotives in that the two prongs of the staple make contact with a pair of metal hollows, which, like the paired rails under the wheels of the train, forces them to follow a preset path, and that they were like phonograph tonearms in that both machines, roughly the same size, make sharp points of contact with their respective media of informational storage. (In the case of the tonearm, the stylus retrieves the information, while in the case of the stapler, the staple binds it together as a unit—the order, the shipping paper, the invoice: *boom*, stapled, a unit; the letter of complaint, the copies of canceled checks and receipts, the letter of apologetic response: *boom*, stapled, a unit; a sequence of memos and telexes holding the history of some interdepartmental controversy: *boom*, stapled, one controversy. In old stapled problems, you can see the TB vaccine marks in the upper left corner where staples have been removed and replaced, removed and replaced, as the problem—even the staple holes of the problem—was copied and sent on to other departments for further action, copying, and stapling.) And then the great era of squareness set in: BART was the ideal for trains, while AR and Bang & Olufsen turntables became angular—no more cream-colored bulbs of plastic! The people at Bates and Swingline again were drawn along, ridding their devices of all softening curvatures and offering black rather than the interestingly textured tan. And now, of course, the high-speed trains of France and Japan have reverted to aerodynamic profiles reminiscent of *Popular Science* cities-of-the-future covers of the fifties; and soon the stapler will incorporate a toned-down pompadour swoop as well. Sadly, the tonearm's stylistic progress has slowed, because all the buyers who would appreciate an up-to-date Soviet Realism in the design are buying CD players: its inspirational era is over.

held up; then, *second*, the moment when the small independent unit in the stapler arm noses into the paper
and begins to force the two points of the staple into
and through it; and, *third*, the felt crunch, like the
chewing of an ice cube, as the twin tines of the staple
emerge from the underside of the paper and are bent
by the two troughs of the template in the stapler's base,
curving inward in a crab's embrace of your memo, and
finally disengaging from the machine completely—

but finding, as you lean on the stapler with your elbow
locked and your breath held and it slumps toothlessly to
the paper, that it has run out of staples. How could something this consistent, this incremental, betray you? (But
then you are consoled: you get to reload it, laying bare the
stapler arm and dropping a long zithering row of staples
into place; and later, on the phone, you get to toy with
the piece of the staples you couldn't fit into the stapler,
breaking it into smaller segments, making them dangle on
a hinge of glue.)

In the aftermath of the broken-shoelace disappointment, irra-
tionally, I pictured Dave, Sue, and Steve as I had just seen
them and thought, "Cheerful assholes!" because I had probably broken the shoelace by transferring the social energy
that I had had to muster in order to deliver a chummy "Have
a good one!" to them from my awkward shoe-tier's crouch
into the force I had used in pulling on the shoelace. Of
course, it would have worn out sooner or later anyway. It was
the original shoelace, and the shoes were old ones my father
had bought me two years earlier, just after I had started this

job, my first out of college—so the breakage was a sentimental milestone of sorts. I rolled back in my chair to study the damage, imagining the smiles on my three co-workers' faces suddenly vanishing if I had really called them cheerful assholes, and regretting this burst of ill feeling toward them.

As soon as my gaze fell to my shoes, however, I was reminded of something that should have struck me the instant the shoelace had first snapped. The day before, as I had been getting ready for work, my *other* shoelace, the right one, had snapped, too, as I was yanking it tight to tie it, under very similar circumstances. I repaired it with a knot, just as I was planning to do now with the left. I was surprised—more than surprised—to think that after almost two years my right and left shoelaces could fail less than two days apart. Apparently my shoe-tying routine was so unvarying and robotic that over those hundreds of mornings I had inflicted identical levels of wear on both laces. The near simultaneity was very exciting—it made the variables of private life seem suddenly graspable and law-abiding.

I moistened the splayed threads of the snapped-off piece and swirled them gently into a damp, unwholesome minaret. Breathing steadily and softly through my nose, I was able to guide the saliva-sharpened leader thread through the eyelet without too much trouble. And then I grew uncertain. In order for the shoelaces to have worn to the breaking point on almost the same day, they would have had to be tied almost exactly the same number of times. But when Dave, Sue, and Steve passed my office door, I had been in the middle of tying one shoe—*one shoe only*. And in the course of a normal day it wasn't at all unusual for one shoe to come untied independent of the other. In the morning, of course, you always tied both shoes, but random midday comings-undone would have to have constituted a significant proportion of the total wear on both of these broken laces, I felt—possibly thirty percent. And how could I be positive that this thirty percent was equally distributed—that right and left shoes had come randomly undone over the last two years with the same frequency?

I tried to call up some sample memories of shoe-tying to determine whether one shoe tended to come untied more often than another. What I found was that I did not retain a single specific engram of tying a shoe, or a pair of shoes, that dated from any later than when I was four or five years old, the age at which I had first learned the skill. Over twenty years of empirical data were lost forever, a complete blank. But I suppose this is often true of moments of life that are remembered as major advances: the discovery is the crucial thing, not its repeated later applications. As it happened, the first *three* major advances in my life—and I will list all the advances here—

1. shoe-tying
2. pulling up on Xs
3. steadying hand against sneaker when tying
4. brushing tongue as well as teeth
5. putting on deodorant after I was fully dressed
6. discovering that sweeping was fun
7. ordering a rubber stamp with my address on it to make bill-paying more efficient
8. deciding that brain cells ought to die

—have to do with shoe-tying, but I don't think that this fact is very unusual. Shoes are the first adult machines we are given to master. Being taught to tie them was not like watching some adult fill the dishwasher and then being asked in a kind voice if you would like to clamp the dishwasher door shut and advance the selector knob (with its uncomfortable grinding sound) to Wash. That was artificial, whereas you knew that adults wanted you to learn how to tie your shoes; it was no fun for them to kneel. I made several attempts to learn the skill, but it was not until my mother placed a lamp on the floor so that I could clearly see the dark laces of a pair of new dress shoes that I really mastered it; she explained again how to form the introductory platform knot, which began high in the air as a frail, heart-shaped loop, and shrunk as you pulled the plastic lace-tips down to a short twisted kernel three-eighths of an inch long, and she showed me how to progress from that base to the main cotyledonary string figure, which was, as it turned out, not a true knot but an illusion, a trick that you performed on the lace-string by bending segments of it back on themselves and tightening other temporary bends around them: it looked like a knot and functioned like a knot, but the whole thing was really an amazing interdependent pyramid scheme, which much later I connected with a couplet of Pope's:

> Man, like the gen'rous vine, supported lives;
> The strength he gains is from th'embrace he gives.

Only a few weeks after I learned the basic skill, my father helped me to my second major advance, when he demonstrated thoroughness by showing me how to tighten the rungs of the shoelaces one by one, beginning down at the toe and working up, hooking an index finger under each X, so that by the time you reached the top you were rewarded with surprising lengths of lace to use in tying the knot, and at the same time your foot felt tightly papoosed and alert.

The third advance I made by myself in the middle of a playground, when I halted, out of breath, to tie a sneaker,[1] my mouth on my interesting-smelling knee, a close-up view of anthills and the tread marks of other sneakers before me (the best kind, Keds, I think, or Red Ball Flyers, had a perimeter of asymmetrical triangles, and a few concavities in the center which printed perfect domes of dust), and found as I retied the shoe that I was doing it automatically, without having to concentrate on it as I had done at first, and, more important, that somewhere over the past year since I had first learned the basic moves, I had evidently evolved two little substeps of my own *that nobody had showed me*. In one I held down a temporarily taut stretch of shoelace with the

---

[1]Sneaker knots were quite different from dress knots—when you pulled the two loops tight at the end, the logic of the knot you had just created became untraceable; while in the case of dress-lace knots, you could, even after tightening, follow the path of the knot around with your mind, as if riding a roller coaster. You could imagine a sneaker-shoelace knot and a dress-shoelace knot standing side by side saying the Pledge of Allegiance: the dress-shoelace knot would pronounce each word as a grammatical unit, understanding it as more than a sound; the sneaker-shoelace knot would run the words together. The great advantage of sneakers, though, one of the many advantages, was that when you had tied them tightly, without wearing socks, and worn them all day, and gotten them wet, and you took them off before bed, your feet would display the impression of the chrome eyelets in red rows down the sides of your foot, like the portholes in a Jules Verne submarine.

side of my thumb; in the other I stabilized my hand with a middle finger propped against the side of the sneaker during some final manipulations. The advance here was my recognition that I had independently developed refinements of technique in an area where nobody had indicated there were refinements to be found: I had personalized an already adult procedure.

Chapter Three
from THE MEZZANINE

Progress like that did not come again until I was over twenty. The fourth of the eight advances I have listed (to bring us quickly up to date, before we return to the broken shoelaces) came when I learned in college that L. brushed her tongue as well as her teeth. I had always imagined that toothbrushing was an activity confined strictly to the teeth, possibly the gums—but I had sometimes felt fleeting doubts that cleaning merely those parts of your mouth really attacked the source of bad breath, which I held to be the tongue. I developed the habit of pretending to cough, cupping my hand over my lips to sniff my breath; when the results disturbed me, I ate celery. But soon after I began going out with L., she, shrugging as if it were a matter of common knowledge, told me that she brushed her tongue every day, with her toothbrush. I shivered with revulsion at first, but was very impressed. It wasn't until three years had passed that I too began brushing my own tongue regularly. By the time my shoelaces broke, I was regularly brushing not only my tongue but the roof of my mouth—

and I am not exaggerating when I say that it is a major change in my life.

The fifth major advance was my discovery of a way to apply deodorant in the morning while fully dressed, an incident I will describe in more detail later on, since it occurred on the very morning I became an adult. (In my case, adulthood itself was not an advance, although it was a useful waymark.)

My second apartment after college was the scene of the sixth advance. The bedroom had a wooden floor. Someone at work (Sue) told me that she was depressed, but that she would go home and clean her apartment, because that always cheered her up. I thought, how strange, how mannerist, how interestingly contrary to my own instincts and practices—deliberately cleaning your apartment to alter your mood! A few weeks later, I came home on a Sunday afternoon after staying over at L.'s apartment. I was extremely cheerful, and after a few minutes of reading, I stood up with the decision that I would clean my room. (I lived in a house with four other people, and thus had only one room that was truly mine.) I picked up articles of clothing and threw some papers out; then I asked myself what people like L., or the depressed woman at work, did next. They swept. In the kitchen closet I found a practically new broom (not one of the contemporary designs, with synthetic bristles uniformly cut at an angle, but one just like the kind I had grown up with, with blond smocked twigs bound to a blue handle by perfectly wrapped silver wire) that one of my housemates had bought. I got to work, reminded of a whole chain of subsidiary childhood discoveries, such as putting to use one of my father's shirt cardboards as a dustpan, and bracing the broom with an armpit in order to sweep the dust one-handed onto the shirt cardboard; and I found that the act of sweeping around the legs of the chair and the casters of the stereo cabinet and the corners of the bookcase, outlining them with my curving broom-strokes, as if I were putting each chair leg and caster and doorjamb in quotation marks, made me see these familiar features of my room with freshened receptivity. The phone rang just as I had swept up a final pile of dust, coins, and old earplugs—the moment when the room was at its very cleanest, because the pile that I had just assembled was still there as evidence. It was L. I told her that I was sweeping my room, and that even though I had already been feeling very cheerful, this sweeping was making me wildly cheerful! She said that she had just swept her apartment, too. She said that for her the best moment was sweeping the dust into the dustpan, and getting those ruler-edged gray lines of superfine residue, one after another, diminishing in thickness toward invisibility, but never completely disappearing, as you backed the dustpan up. The fact that we had independently decided to sweep our apartments on that Sunday afternoon after spending the weekend together, I took as a strong piece of evidence that we were right for each other. And from then on when I read things Samuel Johnson said about the deadliness of leisure and the uplifting effects of industry, I always nodded and thought of brooms.

Advance number seven, occurring not long after the Sunday sweep, was occasioned by my ordering a rubber stamp with my name and address on it from an office-supply store, so that I wouldn't have to write out my return address repeatedly when I paid bills. I had dropped some things off at the cleaner's that day, and the day before I had taken some chairs that L. had inherited from an aunt to be recaned by blind people in a distant suburb; I also had written my grandparents, and I had ordered a transcript of a MacNeil-Lehrer show in which an interviewee had said things that represented with particular clarity a way of thinking I disagreed with, and I had sent off to Penguin, just as they suggested in the back of all their paperbacks, for a "complete list of books available"; two days earlier I had dropped off my shoes to be reheeled—it's amazing that heels wear down before the laces snap—and paid several bills (which had made me think of the need for an address stamp). As I walked out of the office-supply store, I became aware of the power of all these individual, simultaneously pending transactions: all over the city, and at selected sites in other states, events were being set in motion on my behalf, services were being performed, simply because I had requested them and in some cases paid or agreed to pay later for them. (The letter to my grandparents didn't exactly fit, but contributed to the feeling even so.) Molten rubber was soon to be poured into backward metal letters that spelled my name and address; blind people were making clarinetists' finger motions over the holes of a half-caned chair, gauging distances and degrees of tautness; somewhere in the Midwest in rooms full of Tandem computers and Codex statistical multiplexers the magnetic record of certain debts in my name was being overwritten with a new magnetic record that corresponded to a figure diminished to the penny by the amount that I had written out in hasty felt-tip pen on my checks (I made the traditional long wavy mark after "and 00/100" on the dollar line, just as my parents had, and their parents had before them); the dry cleaner's would close soon, and in a sack somewhere in the darkened store, tied in a bundle to keep it separate from all other bundles, behind the faded posters in the window saying "For That Newly Tailored Look," my dirty clothing would rest for the night; I trusted them to take temporary possession of it, and they trusted me to return to their store and pay them for making it look like new. All of this and more I could get the world to do for me, and at the same time all of it was going on, I could walk down the street, unburdened with the niceties of the individual tasks, living my life! I felt like an efficient short-order cook, having eight or nine different egg orders working at once, dropping the toast, rolling the sausages, setting up the plates, flicking the switch that illuminated a waitress's number. It was the rubber stamp specifically that pushed the advance over the top, because, in bearing my name, the stamp summed up all of this action at a distance, and was itself a secondary, life-ordering act, which had taken time now, but which would save time later, *every bill I paid*.

The eighth advance, the last one that I can think of ante-dating the day of the broken laces, was a set of four reasons why it was a good thing for brain cells to die. One way or another, I had worried about the death of brain cells since I was about ten, convinced year after year that I was getting more stupid; and when I began to drink in a small way, and the news broke (while I was in college) that an ounce of distilled spirits kills one thousand neurons (I think that was the ratio), the concern intensified. One weekend I confessed to my mother on the phone that I had been worrying that over the past six months especially, my brain wattage had dimmed perceptibly. She had always been interested in materialist analogies for cognition, and she offered reassurance, as I knew she would. "It's true," she said, "that your individual brain cells are dying, but the ones that stay grow more and more connections, and those connections keep branching out over the years, and that's the progress you have to keep in mind. It's the number of links that are important, not the raw number of cells." This observation was exceedingly helpful. In the week or two following her news that connections continued to proliferate in the midst of neural carnage, I formed several related theories:

(a) We begin, perhaps, with a brain that is much too crowded with pure processing capacity, and therefore the death of the brain cells is part of a *planned and necessary* winnowing that precedes the move upward to higher levels of intelligence: the weak ones fizzle out, and the gaps they leave as they are reabsorbed stimulate the growth buds of dendrites, which now have more capacious playgrounds, and complex correlational structures come about as a result. (Or perhaps the dendrites' own heightened need for space to grow forces a mating struggle: they lock antlers with feebler outriggers in the search for the informationally rich connections, shortcutting through intermediate territories and causing them to wither and shut down like neighborhoods near a new thruway.) With fewer total cells, but more connections between each cell, the quality of your knowledge undergoes a transformation: you begin to have a feel for situations, people fall into types, your past memories link together, and your life begins to seem, as it hadn't when you were younger, an inevitable thing composed of a million small failures and successes dependently intergrown, as opposed to a bright beadlike row of unaffiliated moments. Mathematicians need all of those spare neurons, and their careers falter when the neurons do, but the rest of us should be thankful for their disappearance, for it makes room for experience. Depending on where on the range you began, you are shifted as your brain ages toward the richer, more mingled pole: mathematicians become philosophers, philosophers become historians, historians become biographers, biographers become college provosts, college provosts become political consultants, and political consultants run for office.

(b) Used with care, substances that harm neural tissue, such as alcohol, can aid intelligence: you corrode the chromium, giggly, crossword puzzle-solving parts of your mind with pain and poison, forcing the neurons to take responsibility for themselves and those around them, toughening themselves against the accelerated wear of these artificial solvents. After a night of poison, your brain wakes up in the morning saying, "No, I don't give a shit who introduced the sweet potato into North America." The damage that you have inflicted heals over, and the scarred places left behind have unusual surface areas, roughnesses enough to become the nodes around which wisdom weaves its fibrils.

(c) The neurons that do expire are the ones that made imitation possible. When you are capable of skillful imitation, the sweep of choices before you is too large; but when your brain loses its spare capacity, and along with it some agility, some joy in winging it, and the ambition to do things that don't suit it, then you finally have to settle down to do well the few things that your brain really can do well—the rest no longer seems pressing and distracting, because it is now permanently out of reach. The feeling that you are stupider than you were is what finally interests you in the really complex subjects of life: in change, in experience, in the ways other people have adjusted to disappointment and narrowed ability. You realize that you are no prodigy, your shoulders relax, and you begin to look around you, seeing local color unrivaled by blue glows of algebra and abstraction.

(d) Individual ideas are injured along with the links over which they travel. As they are dismembered and remembered, damaged, forgotten, and later refurbished, they become subtler, more hierarchical, tiered with half-obliterated particulars. When they molder or sustain damage, they regenerate more as a part of the self, and less as a part of an external system.

These were the eight main advances I had available to bring to bear on my life on the day I sat repairing the second shoelace to wear out in two days.

from VOX

"What are you wearing?" he asked.

She said, "I'm wearing a white shirt with little stars, green and black stars, on it, and black pants, and socks the color of the green stars, and a pair of black sneakers I got for nine dollars."

"What are you doing?"

"I'm lying on my bed, which is made. That's an unusual thing. I made my bed this morning. A few months ago my mother gave me a chenille bedspread, exactly the kind we used to have, and I felt bad that it was still folded up unused and this morning I finally made the bed with it."

"I don't know what chenille is," he said. "It's some kind of silky material?"

"No, it's cotton. Cotton chenille. It's got those little tufts, in conventional patterns. Like in bed-and-breakfasts."

"Oh oh oh, the patterns of *tufts*. I'm relieved."

"Why?" she asked.

"Silk is somehow . . . you think of ads for escort services where the type is set in fake-o eighteenth-century script—

For the Discriminating Gentleman—that kind of thing. Or Deliques Intimates, you know that catalog?"

"I get one about every week."

"Right, a deluge. Lace filigree, Aubrey Beardsley, no thank
you. All I can think of is, ma'am, those silk tap pants you've
got on are going to stain."

"You're right about that," she said. "Someone gave me
this exotic chemisey thing, not from Deliques but the same
idea, silk with lace. I get quite . . . I get very *moist* when I'm
aroused, it's almost embarrassing actually. So this chemisey
thing got soaked. He said, the person who bought it for me
said, 'So what, throw it away, use it once.' But I don't know,
I thought I might want to wear it again. It's really nice to
wear silk, you know. So I took it to the dry cleaners. I didn't
mention it specifically, I bunched it in with a lot of work
clothes. It came back with a little tag on it, with a little
dancing man with a tragic expression, wearing a hat, who
says, you know, 'Sorry! We did everything we could, we
took extraordinary measures, but the stains on this garment
could not come out!' I took a look at it, and it was very odd,
there were these five *dot* stains on it, little ovals, not down
where I'd been wet, but higher up, on the front."

"Weird."

"And the guy who gave it to me had *not* come on me. He
came elsewhere—that much I was sure of. So my theory is
that someone at the dry cleaners. . ."

"No! Do you still give them your business?"

"Well, they're convenient."

"Where do you live?"

"In an eastern city."

"Oh. I live in a western city."

"How nice."

"It is nice," he said. "From my window I can see a street-light with lots of spike holes in it, from utility workers—I mean a wooden telephone pole with a streetlight on it—"

"Of course."

"And a few houses. The streetlight is photo-activated, and watching it come on is really one of the most beautiful things."

"What time is it there?"

"Um—six-twelve," he said.

"Is it dark there yet?"

"No. Is it there?"

"Not completely," she said. "It doesn't feel really dark to me until the little lights on my stereo receiver are the brightest things in the room. That's not strictly true, but it sounds good, don't you think? What hand are you holding the phone with?"

"My left," he said.

"What are you doing with your right hand?"

"My right hand is, at the moment, my fingers are resting in the soil of a potted plant somebody gave me, that isn't doing too well. I'm sort of moving my fingers in the soil."

"What kind of a plant?"

"I can't remember," he said. "The soil has several round polished stones stuck in it. Oh wait, here's the tag. No, that's just the price tag. An anonymous mystery plant."

"You haven't told me what *you're* wearing," she said.

"I am wearing . . . I'm wearing, well, a bathrobe, and flip-flops with blue soles and red holder-onners. I'm new to flip-flops—I mean since moving out here. They're good in the morning for waking up. On weekends I put them on and I walk down to the corner and buy the paper, and the feeling of that thong right in the crotch of your toe—man, it pulls you together, it starts your day. It's like putting your feet in a bridle."

"Are you 'into' feet?" she asked.

"No no no no no no no no. On women? No. They're neutral. They're about like elbows. In my *own* case, I do . . ."

"What?"

"Well, I do very often, when I'm about to come, I seem to like to rise up on the balls of my feet. It's something about the tension of all the leg muscles and the, you know, the ass muscles, it puts all the nerves in communication, it's as if I'm coming with my legs. On the other hand, when I do it I sometimes feel like some kind of high school teacher, bouncing on his heels, or like some kind of demagogue, rising up on tiptoe and roaring out something about destiny."

"And then, at the very top of your *relevé*, you come into a tissue," she said.

"Yep."

"The things we do for love. I knew this person, a doctor, who once told me that he liked to hyperventilate when he was masturbating, like a puppy. He got very scientific about it. He said that hyperventilating decreases the ionized calcium in the blood, alters neural conductivity, does this, does that. I tried it once. He said when you're almost there, after panting and panting, he-a-he-a-he-a, you're supposed to do this thing called a Valsalva, which is where you take a breath and you clamp your throat shut and push *hard*, and if you do

it right, you're supposed to have a mind-blowing orgasm—
tingling extremities, tingling roots of your hair, tingling teeth,
I don't know, the whole business. I didn't have much success
with the technique, but he was this huge man, huge coarse
beard, huge arms, he loved large meatball subs, with that
orange grease—and he was so big and so innocent and actually quite shy that the idea of him gasping—"

"His eyes squinted shut."

"Right, hunched over his male organ, though I have to
say I was never quite able to picture his male organ, but the
idea of him intentionally, deliberately gasping and swallow-
ing was enough to help me toward a moment or two of
pleasure myself."

"Ooo. On that very bed?"

"On this very bed."

"But without the chenille bedspread."

"Without the chenille bedspread, which I notice is leaving little white pieces of fluff on my pants, mm, mm, mm,
get off, you. You see, a pretentiously sexy silk bedspread
from Deliques would have been more practical after all."

"Well, right, no, I can see that the things in Deliques might
be sexy," he said. "Garters and all that. They don't do much
for me—in fact, the whole Victorian flavor of a certain kind
of smirky kinkiness puts me off—but still, I have to admit that
when the catalogs started coming, week after week, early fall,
midfall, late fall, this persistent gush of half-dressed women
flowing toward me in the mail, on such expensive paper, with
the bee-stung lips and all that, it did start to interest me."

"Ah, now you're admitting it," she said. "The male models are quite good-looking, too."

"Well, but still for me it wasn't the lace hemi-demi-camisoles or any of that. I'll tell you what it was, in fact. It was this one picture of a woman wearing a loose green shirt, lying on her back, with her legs in the air, crossed at the ankles, wearing a pair of tights. Not black tights. I was, I was absolutely entranced by this picture. I remember coming home from work and sitting at the kitchen table, studying this picture for about . . . ten minutes, reading the little description of the tights, looking at the picture again, reading, looking. She had very long legs. Now, did I have anybody I could buy these tights for? No, not really. Not at that moment. They were made of a certain kind of stitch, not chenille, not chenille. Pointelle! She was wearing these beigey-green pointelle tights. See, to me the word 'tights' is much more exciting than just 'stockings.' Anyway I went into the living room and put the phone on the floor, and then I lay down on the floor next to the phone and I just studied this shot, went through the rest of the catalog, but back to this one picture again, until my arms started to get tired from holding the pages in the air, and I put the catalog facedown on my chest, and I went into a state of pure bliss, rolling my head back and forth on the rug. If you roll your head back and forth on the floor it usually increases any feeling of awe or wonder that you've got going. But no tingling of the extremities, unfortunately."

"No."

"And I don't eat lots of meatball subs. I mean I *do* enjoy a meatball sub occasionally, with mushrooms—I just want to differentiate myself from, you know . . ."

"Oh don't worry about that," she said. "Your accent is very different from his, your voice is quite . . . compelling."

"I'm glad to hear that. I was nervous when I called. My temperature dropped about fifteen degrees as I was deciding to dial the number."

"Really. Where did you see the ad?"

"Ah, a men's magazine."

"Which one?" she asked.

"This is oddly embarrassing. *Juggs*. *Juggs* magazine. Where did you see the ad?"

There was a pause. *"Forum."*

"What does your ad say?" he asked.

"Let me see," she said. "There's a line drawing of a man and a woman, each holding a telephone, and the headline is ANYTIME AT ALL. I liked the drawing."

"I've seen that one," he said. "That's very different from my ad. My ad has a color shot of a woman with a phone cord wrapped around her leg and one arm kind of covering her breasts, and the headline over the phone number is, MAKE IT HAPPEN. But there *is* something intangibly classier about this ad than the other ads, something about the layout and the type that the phone number is in, despite the usual woman-plus-phone image, and I thought that maybe it might attract a different sort of caller. Although, boy, that flurry of assholic horniness from the men on the line when you first spoke was not exactly cucumber sandwich conversation. That *one* guy that kept interrupting—'You like to *sock* on a big *caulk*?' 'How big and brown are your nips?' But then, I suppose we aren't calling for cucumber sandwich conversation."

"I wouldn't object—cucumber away. But I guess not. Anyhow, here we are, 'one on one,' as they say, in the famous fiber-optical 'back room.'"

"True enough."

"So go on," she said. "You were telling me how you were on the floor rolling your head back and forth?"

"Oh, right. Well, I was on the floor with the catalog face-down on my chest, entranced by those tights, and a conception, this conception of thrilling wrongness, took shape in my brain stem. I had a vision of myself jerking off while I ordered that pair of tights, specifically the vision was of, of, of . . ."

"Of?"

"Of being in the bathtub, but on the phone with the order-taker from Deliques, who's got, you know, this nice innocent voice, a mistaken but lovable overfrizzed perm, a hint of twang, bland face, freshly laundered jeans, cute socks, but probably wearing a pair of Deliques finest 'fusion panties' with a chevron of lace or something over her mound, which she's bought at the employee discount, while I'm in my bathtub, which is ridiculous since I never take baths, but I'm in my bathtub moving *so* carefully so she won't hear any aquatic splips or splaps and know that I've taken the portable phone into the bathroom and that I'm semi-submerged, and she says, 'Let me check to be sure we have that in stock for you, sir,' and during the pause, I arch myself up out of the water and sort of point the phone at my Werner Heisenberg so she can see it somehow or get its vibes, and at the moment she says, 'Yes, we do have the pointelle tights in faun,' I come, in perfect silence, making a Smurf grimace."

"That's awful."

"I know, but I don't know, I was there on the living-room floor. I don't often lie down there."

"Were you actually . . . playing with yourself as you envisioned this?"

"Certainly not! I had one hand on the telephone, just *toying* with the number keys, teasing them, and the other hand was lying on the facedown catalog on my chest. Anyway, then I thought I would be embarrassed to order a pair of tights for myself—maybe the order-taker would assume that I was a transsexual, when in fact I am not a transsexual at all, I'm a telephone clitician."

"An obscene phone caller."

"Exactly. And I started to think of who I could order them for, and I thought of this woman at work, a very nice woman, some might say plain, but very nice, who once startled me and this other guy by telling a story out of the blue about some friends of hers who'd just had a large wedding at a museum during which some thieves backed a van up and loaded all the wedding gifts in and drove away."

"The wedding gifts were on display?" she asked.

"Yes."

"Ah, well, that was their mistake."

"Well, they were punished for it. Anyway, one of the gifts, this woman from work told us, was one of those sex slings that I guess you bolt to a stud in the ceiling, so that the woman is . . ."

"Yeah, I know," she said.

"And this woman from work had joked about the difficulty of trying to fence the stolen sex sling, and the memory of her talking about this oddball device came back to me and I wanted to order the tights for her, so she'd come home from work one day, and she'd go, 'Hey, what's this, a slim little package for me from Deliques?' She'd open it up and slip out this plastic packet with tights in it, and there's the order slip in her hand, and somehow I've convinced the order-taker that I don't want my name on the slip."

"Sure, sure."

"So she knows she's got a secret admirer. And there on the packing slip is the line of printout that says, all in abbreviations, I PR PTL TIGHTS, FN, SM, $12.95, and I just thought of her looking at the packing slip and thinking, Well, gee, I suppose I *should* at least see if they fit."

"Ah, but wait," she said. "No, what catches her eye, what catches her eye is. . ."

"Tell me," he said.

"Is that on the packing slip, over the numeral one, for one pair of tights, is this *check mark*, in blunt pencil."

"That's right, there is."

"And she looks closely at that check mark, and she imagines a male hand making it, a surprisingly refined hand, because there has been a strike at the Deliques warehouse, and what's happened is that Deliques management has had to hire the male models from the catalog on an emergency basis to fill in for the normal pickers and packers, who are of course mostly middle-aged Laotian women. And they were right in the middle of a catalog shoot, all these male models, when the walkout took place, so they're wearing exactly what they were wearing on the shoot, which are the usual aubergine paisley boxer shorts, and Henri Rousseau bathrobes, and Erté pajamas, and that sort of thing, but there was no time for them to change, they had to be herded barefoot into this giant warehouse because the company was bombed with orders. April was their biggest month. So—one male model takes this woman's order slip, and studies it, looks at her name on it—what's her name?"

"Jill."

"Looks at her name, Jill Smith, and then takes the order slip and crumples it against the piece of horseradish in his foulard silk boxer shorts, and he hands it to the next male model, a gorgeous peasant with strange slitty nipples, who smoothes it out, studies it, duh, Jill Smith, squeezes his asscheeks together, and passes it to the next guy, who smooths it out, studies it, bites one corner, and hands it to the next guy, and so on down this row of male models, each one broader-shouldered and sinewier-stomached than the last, until finally the order slip gets to the last guy, who's fallen asleep sitting on one tang of the forklift, a much slighter gentleman, with a beautiful throat with a softly pulsing jugular you just wanted to *eat* it looked so good, and of course wearing a green moiré silk codpiece, pushed forward and upward by the one tang of the forklift. This male model rouses himself, smacks his lips sleepily, studies the slip of paper, gets in the forklift, and drives off, weaves off, toward the distant vault where they keep the pointelle tights."

"Yes?"

"And he reaches the mountain of crates marked FAUN, and he slides the forklift into the highest pallet and lifts it off and, *vvvvvvv*, brings it down, and he pries it open . . ."

"Probably with his dick."

"No, no, with his powerful refined *hands*," she said. "The packing tape goes *pap! pap! pap!* as he tears the mighty box asunder. But now that you mention it, as he's reaching in, deep into the box filled with . . . with one metric ton of cotton pointelle, his cock *is* pressing against the cardboard, pressing, pressing, and it starts to fight against the tethers of that codpiece. So he climbs back in the forklift, puts the pair of tights in his lap, and drives back. Well, while he was gone, Todd, Rod, Sod, and Wadd, the other male models, all heterosexual, of course, who've been standing in a row waiting for him, have been thinking about Jill Smith wearing those tights and by now their bobolinks have all gotten thoroughly hard, and even the sleepy forklift driver, perhaps because of the faun tights in his lap, is embarrassed to get out because there's this frank erection that has now gotten so big and bone-hard that it's angling right out of his codpiece. He takes his place in the row of male models, his cock swaying slightly, and he holds the tights to his face and exhales through them, then nods, takes a pencil with a surprisingly sharp point, and makes a check mark over the numeral one on the packing slip. He hands it to the next guy—by this time all the male models have abandoned their shame in each other's presence and they are all standing there in a row with their various organs pronging at various angles out of their various robes and boxers and sex-briefs. So the forklift guy hands it to the next guy, who almost ritualistically takes the tights and winds them around and around his cock, pulls once hard, and then unwinds them and makes a check mark exactly superimposed over the first check mark on the numeral one on the packing slip. And he hands the tights to the next guy, who also winds the tights around his cock, many winds, it's *very* long, and he pulls, and he makes a superimposing check mark, too, and so on down the row, wind unwind check, wind unwind check, and the final guy folds the tights up with neat agile movements that belie his enormous forearms and slides them into the sheer plastic envelope and puts the last check mark over the numeral one, so that it now looks as if only one blunt pencil checkmarked over it, when really there were *nine* check marks. And so together, humming 'The Volga Boatman' in unison, they seal the package up with Jill Smith's address on it and send it off to her."

"Well, maybe that *is* what happened," he said. "No, in reality, there wasn't any strike at Deliques when I called. Their computer was down, though.

"Oh, so you really *did* call?" she said. "That's very wicked of you. In the bath?"

"No, in the end that seemed like too much trouble. I called from the living-room floor. First I worked myself up to a creditable state of engorgement, then I dialed the 800 number."

"All right . . ."

"A woman answered and said something like 'Hello and welcome to Deliques Intimates, this is Clititia speaking, how may we help you today?' She had a young high voice, exactly the sort of voice I'd imagined. Well, my fourteen-and-a-half-inch sperm-dowel instantly shrank to less than three inches. Which is the opposite of what was supposed to happen. I told her what I wanted to order, and she said the computer was down, but she would take the order 'by hand,'

right? Why wasn't I enough of a leerer to come back with
something insinuating? Just something basic, like 'Heh heh,
honey, I hope you *do* take it all by hand.' But instead I just
said, 'Boy oh boy, that must be a lot of trouble for you.' I
gave her my address, my card number, and she said, 'I've got
that, sir, now, is there anything else you would like to order
this evening?' I said, 'Well, I'm torn, there *is* one other thing
I'd like to get this person, just a pair of very simple panties,
but I'm torn.' I said, 'Now you see the so-called Deliques
minimes on page thirty-eight? You see those? Do you have
the catalog there right in front of you?' She said she did. I
said, 'Okay. I'm not sure I can tell the difference between
these *minimes* and the so-called *nadja pants* on page, ah, forty-
six. To the naked eye they seem identical.' She said, 'Just one
moment,' and I heard her flipping through the catalog, and
I made a last valiant attempt to stroke myself off, because the
idea of her looking carefully at those pictures of women in
those tiny weightless panties, with the darkness of pubic hair
visible right *there* through the material, at the very same time
I was looking at those same cuppable curves of pubic hair
on my end, should have been enough to make me shoot
instantly, but I don't know, she sounded so well-meaning,
and I knew that there was a very good chance that she would
not like to know that I was there trying to . . . I mean, she
didn't want to work at a job where men called her and
ordered a few items of merchandise just so they could . . .
right? That wasn't what she'd had in mind at all in taking the
job, or possibly wasn't, at least, so even when she said, finally,
'Well, the nadja pants ride a little lower on the hip,' which is
a statement that any normal jacker-offer should be able to

come to easily, because what does it imply? It implies her own hip, it implies that the nadja panties have ridden *her own hip*. But even then I could not achieve and maintain. So I said, 'Oh well, no, thanks, I'll see how the tights go over and then order the *minimes* later.' And a week afterward, I was the owner of a pair of tights. I still have them, unopened. Give me your address and I'll be glad to forward them to you."

"Why don't you give them to Jill?" she asked.

"Oh, a million reasons. But that's not quite the end. I hung up from making the order and instantly I got hard again, naturally, and I thought for a second, and I hit the redial button, and a different woman answered, with a much lower and smarter voice, with some name like Vulva, and I said, 'Vulva, I have what may sound like an unorthodox question, and you don't have to answer it if you don't want to. But what I'm curious about is, well, of the men who order from your catalog, do you think some of them are in a subtle and maybe not-so-subtle way obscene phone callers?' She laughed and she said, 'That's a good question.' And then there was a long pause, a very long pause. I said, 'Hello?' And right there I knew I'd blown it—I knew the tone of my hello, that slight reediness in my voice that betrayed sexual tension, blew away the potential rapport I might have had with Vulva. See, I'd sounded quite confident when I actually asked her the question."

"What did she say?"

"She just said, in a more official voice, but still a friendly voice, 'I don't think I'm going to answer your question.' And I said, 'Fine, I understand, okay, sure.' And she said 'Bye.' Not 'Good-bye,' you notice—still the slight vestige of amused intimacy there. If she'd said 'Good-bye' I would have felt absolutely crushed."

"What did you do then?"

"I sat up and ordered a pizza and read the paper. So you see, I'm not an obscene phone caller, really. I can't smother an orgasm."

"Ho ho. I can," she said.

"Can you? Well, I mean I can physically do it."

"*I* know what you mean."

There was a pause.

"I hear ice cubes," he said.

"Diet Coke."

"Ah. Tell me more things. Tell me about the room you're in. Tell me the chain of events that led up to your calling this number."

"Okay," she said. "I'm not in the bedroom anymore. I'm sitting on the couch in my living room slash dining room. My feet are on the coffee table, which would have been impossible yesterday, because the coffee table was piled so high with mail and work stuff, but now it is possible, and the whole room, the whole apartment, is really and truly in order. I took a sick day today, without being sick, which is something I haven't done up to now at this job. I called the receptionist and told her I had a fever. The moment of lying to her was awful, but gosh what freedom when I hung up the phone! And I didn't leave the apartment all day. I just organized my immediate surroundings, I picked up things, I vacuumed, and I laid out all the silver that I've inherited— three different very incomplete patterns—laid it out on the dining-room table and looked at it and I gave some serious thought to polishing it, but I didn't go so far as to polish it, but it looked beautiful all laid out, a big arch of forks, a little arch of knives, five big serving spoons, some tiny salt spoons, and a little grouping of novelty items, like oyster forks. No teaspoons at all. One of the dinner forks from my great aunt's set fell into the dishwasher once when I was visiting her and it got badly notched by that twirly splasher in the bottom, and someone at work was telling me he knew a jeweler who fixed hurt silverware, so I'm planning to have that fixed, it's all ready to go. And I even got together all my broken sets of beads—I sorted them all out—the sight of all those beads jumbled together on my bedside table was making me unhappy every morning, and now they're ready to be restrung, the pink ones in one envelope, and the green ones in one envelope, and the parti-colored Venetian ones in one envelope—and I have them on my dining-room table too, ready to go."

"The same jeweler who fixes silverware restrings beads?" he asked.

"Yes!"

"How did your beads get broken?"

"They seem to break in the morning when I'm rushing to get dressed. They catch on something. The jade ones, my favorite set, which my father gave me, caught on the open door of the microwave when I was standing up too quickly after picking a piece of paper up off the floor. That was the latest tragedy. And of course my sister's babe yanked one set off my neck. But they can all be repaired and they will all be repaired."

"Good going."

"Anyway, this apartment is transformed, I mean it, not just superficially but with new hidden pockets of order in it, and I waited until the midafternoon to have a shower, and I did *not* masturbate, because the illicitness of calling in sick without justification made me want to be pure and virtuous all day long, and I had an early dinner of Carr's Table Water crackers with cream cheese and sliced pieces of sweet red kosher peppers on them, just delicious, and I did *not* turn on the TV but instead I turned on the stereo, which I haven't used much lately. It's a very fancy stereo."

"Yes?"

"I think I spent something like fourteen hundred dollars on it," she said. "I bought it from someone who was buying an even fancier system. It was true insanity. I had a crush on this person. He liked the Thompson Twins and the S.O.S. Band and, gee, what were the other groups he liked so much? The Gap Band was one. Midnight Star. And Cameo. This was a while ago. He was not a particularly intelligent man, in fact in a way he was a very dimwitted narrow-minded man, but he was *so* infectiously convinced that what he liked everyone would like if they were exposed to it. And good-looking. For about four months, while I was in his thrall, I really *listened* to that stuff. I gave my life up to it. My own taste in music stopped evolving in grade school with the Beatles, the early early Beatles—in fact I used to dislike any song that didn't end—you know, end with a chord, but simply faded out."

"But then you met this guy," he said.

"Exactly!" she said. "All of the songs he liked faded out, or most of them did. And so I became a connoisseur of fade-

outs. I bought cassettes. I used to turn them up very loud—
with the headphones on—and listen very closely, trying to
catch that precise moment when the person in the record-
ing studio had begun to turn the volume dial down, or
whatever it was he did. Sometimes I'd turn the volume dial
up at just the speed I thought he—I mean the ghostly hand
of the record producer—was turning it down, so that the
sound stayed on an even plane. I'd get in this sort of trance,
like you on the rug, where I thought if I kept turning it
up—and this is a very powerful amplifier, mind you—the
song would not stop, it would just continue indefinitely.
And so what I had thought of before as just a kind of artistic sloppiness, this attempt to imply that oh yeah, we're a
bunch of endlessly creative folks who jam all night, and the
bad old record producer finally has to turn down the volume on us just so we don't fill the whole album with one
monster song, became for me instead this kind of, this kind
of summation of hopefulness. I first felt it in a song called
'Ain't Nobody,' which was a song that this man I had the
crush on was particularly keen on. *'Ain't nobody, loves me better.'* You know that one?"

"You sing well!" he said.

"I do not. But that's the song, and as you get toward the
end of it, a change takes place in the way you hear it, which
is that the knowledge that the song is going to end starts to
be more important than the specific ups and downs of the
melody, and even though the singer is singing just as loud as
ever, in fact she's really pouring it on now, she's fighting to
be heard, it's as if you are hearing the inevitable waning of
popularity of that hit, its slippage down the charts, and the

twilight of the career of the singer, despite all of the beautiful subtle things she's able to do with a plain old dumb old
bunch of notes, and even as she goes for one last high note,
full of daring and hope and passionateness and everything
worthwhile, she's lost, she's sinking down."

"Oh! Don't *cry!*" he said. "I'm not equipped . . . I mean
my comforting skills don't have that kind of range."

There was another sound of ice cubes. She said, "It's just
that I really liked him. Vain bum. We went dancing one night,
and I made the mistake of suggesting to him as we were on
the dance floor that maybe he should take his pen out of his
shirt pocket and put it in his back pocket. And that was it,
he never called me again."

"That little scum-twirler! Tell me his address, I'll fade *him*
out, I'll rip his arms off."

"No. I got over it. Anyway, that wasn't what I meant to talk
about. I just mean I was here in my wonderfully orderly
apartment after dinner and I saw this big joke of a stereo system and I switched it on, and the sky got darker and all the
little red and green lights on the receiver were like ocean
buoys or something, and I started to feel what you'd expect,
sad, happy, resigned, horny, some combination of all of them,
and I felt suddenly that I'd been virtuous for long enough and
probably should definitely masturbate, and I thought wait,
let's not just have a perfunctory masturbation session, Abby,
let's do something just a little bit special tonight, to round out
a special day, right? So I brought out a copy of *Forum* that I
rather bravely bought one day a while ago. But I'd read all the
stories and all the letters and it just wasn't working. So I

started looking at the ads, really almost for the first time. And there was this headline: ANYTIME AT ALL."

"MAKE IT HAPPEN."

"That's right. And I *like* the sound of the pauses in long-distance conversations—the cassette hiss sound. And yet I didn't really want to talk to anyone I knew. So that's more or less why I called. Now I've answered your questions, now you tell me something."

"Do you want to hear something true, or something imaginary?"

"First true, then imaginary," she said.

"Once," he said, "I was listening to the stereo with the headphones on, I was about sixteen, and the stereo receiver was on the floor of a little room off the living room, I don't know why it was on the floor, I guess because my father was repainting the living room—that must have been it—and the headphone cord was quite short, but I was very interested in learning how to dance. It was winter, it was maybe eight o'clock at night, very dark, I hadn't turned on the light in the room. And I was trying to learn all these moves, but tethered to the stereo, so I was almost completely doubled over, like I was tracking some animal, but I was really ecstatic—dancing, sweating, out of breath, flailing my arms, doing little jumps . . . once I got a little too excited and did a *big* sideways bob of my head and the headphones came off and pulled my glasses off with them—but no problem, I just stylized the motions of picking up my glasses and putting them on and repeated them a few times, incorporated them in. And then suddenly I hear, 'Jim, *what* are you doing?' in this horrified voice. My younger sister had heard all this breathing and panting coming from me in the darkness and thought of course that I was . . ."

"Right."

"I said, 'I'm dancing.' And she went away. I danced for a while longer, but with somewhat less conviction. That was my year of heavy stereo use. Unlike you I didn't have a big crush on anyone at the time. I think it was more that I had a crush on the tuner itself, frankly. I used to imagine that the megahertz markings were the skyline of a city at night. The FM markings were all the buildings, and the AM markings were their reflection in water . . ."

"Ah," she said, "but you're supposed to be telling me something true, not imagined."

"Yes, but the true thing is shading into the imagined thing, all right? And the little moving indicator on our stereo was lit with a yellow light, and I knew where all the stations were on the dial, and I'd spin the knob and the yellow indicator would glide up and down the radio cityscape like a cab up and down some big central boulevard, and each station was an intersection, in a neighborhood with a different ethnic mix, and if the red sign came on saying STEREO I might idle there for a while, or the cabbie might run the light, passing the whole thing by as it exploded and disappeared behind me. And sometimes I'd thumb the dial very slowly, sort of like I was palming a steering wheel, and move up, move up, in the silence of the muted stretches, and then suddenly I'd pierce the rind of a station and there would be this crackling hopped-up luridly colored version of a song that sounded for a second much better than I knew the song really was, like that moment in solar eclipses when the whole corona is visible, and then you slide down into the fertile valley of the station itself, and it spreads out beneath you, in stereo, with a whole range of middle and misty distances."

"That's true!" she said.

"It *is* true? That's bad, because it means that I still have to come up with an imaginary thing, right?"

"I'm afraid so."

"But my imagination doesn't work that way," he said. "It doesn't just hop to at the snap of a finger. What do you want the imaginary thing I tell you to be about?"

"I think it should be about . . . my beads and my silver-ware, since they're all laid out for us."

"Well," he said. There was a pause. "Once there was a guy who, um, needed his fork repaired. No, I can't. I'm sorry. You tell me something more."

"It's *your* turn."

"I need more confidences from you first. I need to be charged up with a stream of confidences flowing from you to me."

"Come on now," she said. "Give it a try."

"Yeah, but I don't think I can just be handed an assignment like that. I'm pedestrian. I think I have to stay with the truth."

"All right, tell me what the most recent thing or event was that aroused you."

"The idea of making this call," he said.

"Before that."

"Let me think back," he said. "The Walt Disney character of Tinker Bell. I was just leaving the video store, and I

came to this big cardboard display of *Peter Pan*, the Walt Disney cartoon *Peter Pan*, which has just been rereleased, with a
TV beside it playing the movie."

"When was this?"

"This was today, about an hour and a half ago, I guess. I
rented three X-rated tapes."

"And you're going to play them later this evening?"

"Maybe. Maybe not, I don't know. I was going to play
them when I got home."

"The second you got home."

"That's right."

"What about dinner?"

"I ate at a pizza place."

"What kind?"

"Small mushroom anchovy."

"All right. So you got home with the tapes . . ."

"Yeah, and I put them on top of the TV and got out of
my work clothes and put on a bathrobe . . ."

"Just a bathrobe?"

"Well, I have my T-shirt and underwear on underneath,
of course."

"White underwear?"

"Gray, white, somewhere in that range. Anyway, I came
out and saw the pile of X-rated tapes on top of my TV, and
they're in these orange boxes. The store uses brown boxes for
their normal tapes, like adventure, comedy, slasher, etcetera,
and then they use a whole different color, an orange box, for
the adult tapes. It's to avoid confusion, because now there
are so many X-rated Christmas tapes and X-rated versions
of *Cinderella* and all that. And I'd never seen two of these

particular tapes before, but of course I knew what was in them anyway, and I heartily approved of it, I'm enthusiastically pro-pornography, obviously, but suddenly I foresaw my own crude arousal—I saw myself fast-forwarding through the numbing parts, trying to find some image that was good, or at least good enough to come to, and the sound of the VCR as it fast-forwards, that industrial robot sound, and I suddenly thought no, no, even though one of the tapes has got Lisa Melendez in it, who I think is just . . . delightful, I thought no, I don't want to see these right now. Fortunately, I'd also bought a *Juggs* magazine, because this anti-orange-tape reaction has hit me before. There are just times when you want a fixed image."

"There's always the pause button," she suggested.

"Well, but then you get those white sawtooth lines across the screen."

"Four heads are better than two, as they say. Of course, the resolution is better on the magazine page, I imagine."

"It certainly is," he said. "But it's much more than that! Don't laugh, really. No movie still is ever as good as a photograph. A photograph catches a woman at a point where her frans are at their perfect point of expressiveness—the soul of her frans is revealed, or rather the souls *are* revealed, because each has a separate personality. Nipples in still pictures are as varied and as communicative as women's eyes, or almost."

"Frans?"

"Yeah, sometimes I don't like the word 'breasts' and all those slangish synonyms. I mean, just look at the drop in arousingness between *Playboy* magazine and the exact same women when they're *moving* from pose to pose on the *Play-boy* channel. It's true that I don't actually get the *Playboy* channel, so I see everything on it through those hounds-tooth and herringbone cycles of the scrambling circuit, and I keep flipping back and forth between it and the two chan-nels on either side of it because sometimes for an instant the picture is startled into visibility just after you switch the channel, and you'll catch this bright yellow torso and one full fran with a fire-engine-red nipple, and then it teeters, it falters, and collapses—and I've noticed that the scrambling works least well and you can see things best when nothing is moving in the TV image, i.e., when it's a TV image *of* a mag-azine image, sort of as if the scrambling circuitry is overcome in the same way I am sometimes overcome by the power of fixed pictures. I once stayed up until two-thirty in the morn-ing doing this, flipping."

"Anyway."

"Right. Anyway, I looked through my brand-new *Juggs* magazine with high hopes, but I don't know—again, the sexiest woman was in a poolside setting, and I find pool-side settings unerotic—that is to say, in general I find them unerotic, since God knows I've certainly come to an enor-mous number of poolside layouts in magazines, but there's something about the publicness of its being outside, in the sun—it's not as bad as a beach setting, which is a complete turnoff—I mean, again, if I were exiled to a desert island with nothing but some pages of a men's magazine showing a nude woman on a desert island, with the arty kidney shapes of sand on the ass-cheeks and all that, I would probably break down and masturbate to it . . . what do you think of that word?"

" 'Masturbate'? I don't hate it. I don't love it."

"Let's get a new word for it," he said.

"To myself, I sometimes call it 'dithering myself off.' "

"Okay, a possibility. What about just 'fiddle'? Fiddlin' yourself off? The dropped *g* is kind of racy. No, no. *Strum.*"

"Strum."

"That's it. I looked through the *Juggs*, and even though it was a poolside scene, I tried to *strum*, and there *was* one shot where the woman was looking straight at me, on her elbows on a yellow pool raft, and her frans were at their point of perfect beauty, not erect nipples but soft rounded tolerant nipples, which you have to have in a poolside photo set because as soon as you see those erect nipples in a poolside layout you think *cold water*, you don't think arousal. I want you to know, by the way, that I am not one of these sad individuals who hang out at the frozen fried-chicken section of the supermarket where it's extra cold just to see women's nipples get hard. I don't get the least thrill from wet T-shirt contests either, because I have to have an answering arousal there in the woman, and cold water is anti-sexual, except if in the case of the wet T-shirt contest I can convince myself that this woman is using the shock of the cold water, the giggliness and the splutteriness of it, to make something possible that otherwise wouldn't be possible and yet is arousing to her: I mean if she *wants* to show off her breasts, if she's proud of them and yet knows she's not the kind of person who's going to go off and become a stripper or whatever, and the douse of cold water is distracting enough to keep her sense of its all being in innocent fun in the end, *then* I can get turned on by shots of a wet T-shirt contest. You know?"

"I can see how that works. So you're looking at the woman in *Juggs*."

"Yes, and she was looking right at me, so appealingly, with such a lucid joyful amused look and her elbows were really digging into the pillow of the yellow raft, so it looked as if it might burst, and I could almost imagine strumming myself off to this, but then, no, there were too many things wrong—the photographer had put her hair in pigtails, tied with some kind of thick purply pink polyester yarn, and it just seemed so awful somehow, the age-old thing of men wanting to pretend that twenty-eight-year-old women are little girls by forcing this icon of girlishness, pigtails, on them, when really, when was the last time you saw a real little girl wearing pigtails? Not to *mention* the incidental fact that little girls are a turnoff. Here's this beautiful, alert, lovely woman, of at least twenty-seven, and all I could see was the dickhead photographer handing her some polyester yarn and saying, 'Uhright, now tie this purple stuff in your hair.' And I felt at that moment that I wanted to talk to a real woman, no more images of any kind, no fast forward, no pause, no magazine pictures. And there was the ad."

"But you've called these numbers before, haven't you?" she asked.

"A few times, but with no real success. And I don't think I've ever called this very number before—2VOX."

"What do you mean by 'success'?"

"No women with any kind of spark. Or, actually, honestly, few women at all, period, except the ones who are paid by the phone service to make mechanical sexual small talk and moan occasionally. It's mostly just men saying 'Hey, any ladies out there?' But then once in a while a real woman will call. And at least with this, as opposed to pictures, at least there's the remote possibility of something clicking. Perhaps it's presumptuous of me to say that we, you and I, click, but there is that possibility."

"Yes."

"In a way it's like the radio. Do you know that I've never actually gone to a store and bought a record? That's probably why I never learned to appreciate the fade-out, as you describe it, since on the radio, one song melts into the next. But it seems to me that you really need the feeling of radio luck in listening to pop music, since after all it's about somebody meeting, out of all the zillions of people in the world, this one other nice person, or at least several adequate people. And so, if you buy the record, or the tape, then you *control* when you can hear it, when what you want is for it to be like luck, and like fate, and to zoom up and down the dial, looking for the song you want, hoping some station will play it—and the joy when it finally rotates around is so intense. You're not hearing it, you're overhearing it."

"On the other hand," she said, "if you own the tape, you show you've got some self-knowledge: you know what you like, you know how to make yourself happy, you're not just wandering in this welter of chance occurrences, passively hoping the disc jockey will come through. Maybe when you're a little kid you find yourself out on a balcony in the sun and you think, My oh my, this feels unexpectedly nice.

But later on you think, I know that I will feel a particular kind of pleasure if I walk out onto this balcony and sit in that chair, and I wish to experience that pleasure now."

"Well, right, and so the reason I called this line was that the pleasures I'd sought out weren't doing it for me and there was this hope of luck, that I, that there would be a conversation . . ."

"You never said what it was about the Disney Tinker Bell exactly, at the video store."

"Well, in the scene I saw, and this is the first time I've seen any of this particular Disney by the way, and you have to remember that I'm in an altered state there in the movie store, with my three orange movies and my men's magazine in my briefcase, but in the scene, Tinker Bell zips around in a sprightly way, with lots of zings of the xylophone and little sparkly stars trailing her flight, and you think, right, typical fairy image, ho hum. And she's *tiny*, she's a tiny suburbanite, she's about five inches tall. This insubstantial, magical, cutely Walt Disneyish woman. But then this thing happens. She pauses in mid-air, and she looks down at herself, and she's got quite small breasts—"

"I thought you didn't like that word."

"You're right, but sometimes it seems right. Actually most of the time it's the right word. Anyway, she's got quite small breasts but quite *large* little hips, and *large* little thighs, and she's wearing this tiny little outfit that's torn or jaggedly cut and barely covers her, and she looks down at herself, a lovely little pouty face, and she puts her hands on her hips as if to measure them, and she shakes her head sadly—too wide, too wide. *Oh* that got me hot! This tiny sprite with *big hips*. And then a second later she gets caught in a dresser drawer among a lot of sewing things and she tries to fly out the key-hole but—nope, her hips are too wide, she gets stuck!"

"Sounds sizzling hot."

"It was."

"You remember *Gentlemen Prefer Blondes*, when Marilyn Monroe tries to squeeze through a porthole on a ship, but her hips are too wide?"

"I *don't* remember that. I better rent that."

"It would be funny if Tinker Bell inspired old Marilyn," she said. "You know, I found the Disney *Peter Pan* vaguely sexual, too."

"Well, yeah—J. M. Barrie was a fudgepacker from way back, and clearly some of that forbiddenness sneaks into every version."

"The girl floats around in her nightgown," she said. "That interested me quite a bit. And she's *too old* to live in the room with the littler kids—I remember that. I must have been about twelve. I saw it with my friend Pamela, who I think has turned out to be a lesbian, bless her soul. We used to build tents in her bedroom and eat saltines and read the medical encyclopedia together. It showed the dotted lines where the surgeon would cut cartilage from the ears if you were having an operation to make your ears flare out less. And at the end of each entry it would say, it was done in a question-and-answer format, it would say, 'When can marital relations be resumed?' And the answer always was four to six weeks. No matter where the dotted lines were, it seemed you could always resume marital relations after four to six weeks. I used to read the articles aloud to her. And once she

read a whole romance novel aloud to me in one night. I fell
asleep somewhere in the middle and woke up again later—
Pamela was a little hoarse, but she was still reading. And
once, maybe it was that same night, I told her a sexual fantasy I'd had a few times, in which I'm at a place where I'm
told I have to take off all my clothes and get into this tube."

"Sorry, get into what?"

"This tube, a long tube," she said. "I slide in, feet first, and
I begin moving down this very long tube, on some sort of
slow current of oil. I'm sure you remember those water
slides that you set up on the lawn, that destroyed the grass?
This was not as fast-moving as that, much slower-moving,
but no friction, and in a luminous tube. As I went along
these pairs of hands would enter the tube a little ahead of
me, waving around blindly, looking for something to feel,
and then my feet would brush under them, and they would
try to grasp my ankles, but their fingers were dripping with
oil, and as I moved forward they slid up my legs, holding me
quite hard, but without friction because of the oil, and then
they pressed down as my stomach went under them, and
then they sort of turned to encounter my breasts, the two
thumbs were almost touching, and they slid very slowly over
my breasts, pushing them up, and believe me, in this fantasy
I had very large heavy breasts, it took a long time for the
hands to slide over them."

"Wow! What did old Pamela say when you told her that?"

"I finished describing it, and I asked her if she had thoughts
like that and she said 'No!' in quite a shocked voice. She
said, 'No! Tell me another.' You think maybe my tube was
what turned her into a lesbian?"

"Well, it certainly would have turned me into a lesbian. But now—can you clarify one thing for me? Do you right now have the light on or off in the room you're in, the combination living room dining room?"

"I have it on. It's a table lamp. I could turn it off if you'd like."

"Perhaps that, perhaps that would . . ."

"Listen." There was a click.

Chapter One
from THE FERMATA

am going to call my autobiography *The Fermata*, even
though "fermata" is only one of the many names I have for
the Fold. "Fold" is, obviously, another. Every so often, usually
in the fall (perhaps mundanely because my hormone-flows
are at their highest then), I discover that I have the power to
drop into the Fold. A Fold-drop is a period of time of variable length during which I am alive and ambulatory and
thinking and looking, while the rest of the world is stopped,
or paused. Over the years, I have had to come up with various techniques to trigger the pause, some of which have
made use of rocker-switches, rubber bands, sewing needles,
fingernail clippers, and other hardware, some of which have
not. The power seems ultimately to come from within me,
grandiose as that sounds, but as I invoke it I have to believe
that it is external for it to work properly. I don't inquire into
origins very often, fearing that too close a scrutiny will
damage whatever interior states have given rise to it, since it
is the most important ongoing adventure of my life.

I'm in the Fold right now, as a matter of fact. I want first
to type out my name—it's Arnold Strine. I prefer Arno to

the full Arnold. Putting my own name down is loin-girding somehow—it helps me go ahead with this. I'm thirty-five. I'm seated in an office chair whose four wide black casters roll silently over the carpeting, on the sixth floor of the MassBank building in downtown Boston. I'm looking up at a woman named Joyce, whose clothes I have rearranged somewhat, although I have not actually removed any of them. I'm looking directly at her, but she doesn't know this. While I look I'm using a Casio CW-16 portable electronic typewriter, which is powered by four D batteries, to record what I see and think. Before I snapped my fingers to stop the flow of time in the universe, Joyce was walking across the carpeting in a gray-blue knit dress, and I was sitting behind a desk twenty or thirty feet away, transcribing a tape. I could see her hipbones under her dress, and I immediately knew it was the time to Snap in. Her pocketbook is still over her shoulder. Her pubic hair is very black and nice to look at— there is lots and lots of it. If I didn't already know her name, I would probably now open her purse and find out her name, because it helps to know the name of a woman I undress. There is moreover something very exciting, almost moving, about taking a peek at a woman's driver's license without her knowing—studying the picture and wondering whether it was one that pleased her or made her unhappy when she was first given it at the DMV.

But I do know this woman's name. I've typed some of her tapes. The language of her dictations is looser than some of the other loan officers'—she will occasionally use a phrase like "spruce up" or "polish off" or "kick in" that you very seldom come across in the credit updates of large regional banks. One of her more recent dictations ended with something like "Kyle Roller indicated that he had been dealing with the subject since 1989. Volume since that time has been $80,000. He emphatically stated that their service was substandard. He indicated that he has put further business with them on hold because they had 'lied like hell' to him. He indicated he did not want his name mentioned back to the Pauley brothers. This information was returned to Joyce Collier on—" and then she said the date. As prose it is not Penelope Fitzgerald, perhaps, but you crave any tremor of life in these reports, and I will admit that I felt an arrow go through me when I heard her say "lied like hell."

Last week, Joyce was wearing this very same gray-blue hipbone-flaunting dress one day. She dropped off a tape for me to do and told me that she liked my glasses, and I've been nuts about her since. I blushed and thanked her and told her I liked her scarf, which really was a very likable scarf. It had all sorts of golds and blacks and yellows in it, and Cyrillic letters seemed to be part of the design. She said, "Well thank you, I like it, too," and she surprised me (surprised us both possibly) by untying it from her neck and pulling it slowly through her fingers. I asked whether those were indeed Cyrillic letters I saw before me, and she said that they were, pleased at my attentiveness, but she said that she had asked a friend of hers who knew Russian what they spelled, and he had told her that they meant nothing, they were just a jumble of letters. "Even better," I said, somewhat idiotically, anxious to show how completely uninterested I was in her mention of a male friend. "The designer picked the letters for their formal beauty—he didn't try to pretend he knew

the language by using a real word." The moment threatened
to become more flirtatious than either of us wanted. I hurried us past it by asking her how soon she needed her tape
done. (I'm a temp, by the way.) "No big rush," she said. She
retied her scarf, and we smiled quite warmly at each other
again before she went off. I was happy all that day just because
she had told me she liked my glasses.

Joyce is probably not going to play a large part in this
account of my life. I have fallen in love with women many,
many times, maybe a hundred or a hundred and fifty times;
I've taken off women's clothes many times, too: there is nothing particularly unusual about this occasion within which I
am currently parked. The only unusual thing about it is that
this time I'm writing about it. I know there are thousands of
women in the world I could potentially feel love for as I do
feel it now for Joyce—she just happens to work at this office
in the domestic-credit department of MassBank where I
happen to be a temp for a few weeks. But that is the strange
thing about what you are expected to do in life—you are
supposed to forget that there are hundreds of cities, each
one of them full of women, and that it is most unlikely that
you have found the perfect one for you. You are just supposed to pick the best one out of the ones you know and
can attract, and in fact you do this happily—you feel that the
love you direct toward the one you do choose is not arbi-
trarily bestowed.

And it *was* brave and friendly of Joyce to compliment me
that way about my glasses. I always melt instantly when I'm
praised for features about which I have private doubts. I first
got glasses in the summer after fourth grade. (Incidentally,

fourth grade is also the year I first dropped into the Fold—
my temporal powers have always been linked in a way I don't
pretend to understand with my sense of sight.) I wore them
steadily until about two years ago, when I decided that I
should at least try contact lenses. Maybe everything would
be different if I got contacts. So I did get them, and I enjoyed
the rituals of caring for them—caring for this pair of demand-
ing twins that had to be bathed and changed constantly. I
liked squirting the salt water on them, and holding one of
them in an aqueous bead on the tip of my finger and admir-
ing its Saarinenesque upcurve, and when I folded it in half
and rubbed its slightly slimy surface against itself to break up
the protein deposits, I often remembered the satisfactions of
making omelets in Teflon fry-pans. But though as a hobby
they were rewarding, though I was as excited in opening the
centrifugal spin-cleaning machine I ordered for them as I
would have been if I had bought an automatic bread baker
or a new kind of sexual utensil, they interfered with my appreciation of the world. I could see things through them, but I
wasn't *pleased* to look at things. The bandwidth of my optical processors was being flooded with "there is an intruder
on your eyeball" messages, so that a lot of the incidental visual
haul from my retina was simply not able to get through. I
wasn't enjoying the sights you were obviously meant to enjoy,
as when you walked around a park on a windy day watching people's briefcases get blown around on their arms.

At first I thought it was worth losing the beauty of the
world in order to look better to the world: I really was more
handsome without glasses—the dashing scar on my left eye-
brow, where I cut myself on a scrap of aluminum, was more

evident. A girl I knew (and whose clothes I removed) in high school used to sing *"Il faut souffrir pour être belle"* in a soft voice, to a tune of her own devising, and I took that overheard precept seriously; I was willing to understand it not just in the narrow sense of painful hair-brushing or (say) eyebrow-tweezing or liposuction, but in some broader sense that suffering makes for beauty in art, that the artist has to suffer griefs and privations in order to deliver beauty to his or her public, all that well-ventilated junk. So I continued to wear contacts even when each blink was a dry torment. But then I noticed that my *typing* was suffering, too—and there, since I am a temp and typing is my livelihood, I really had to draw the line. Especially when I typed numbers, my error rate was way up. (Once I spent two weeks doing nothing but typing six-digit numbers.) People began bringing back financial charts that I had done with mistyped numbers circled in red, asking, "Are you all right today, Arno?" Contact lenses also, I noticed, made me feel, as loud continuous factory noise also will, ten feet farther away from anyone else around me. They were isolating me, heightening rather than helping rid me of my—well, I suppose it is proper to call it my loneliness. I missed the sharp corners of my glasses, which had helped me dig my way out into sociability; they had been part of what I felt was my characteristic expression.

When I started today, I had no intention of getting into all this about eyeglasses. But it is germane. I love looking at women. I love being able to see them clearly. I particularly like being in the position I am in this very second, which is not looking at Joyce, but rather thinking about the amazing fact that I *can* look up from this page at any time and stare at any part of her that calls out to me for as long as I want without troubling or embarrassing her. Joyce doesn't wear glasses, but my ex-girlfriend Rhody did—and somewhere along the line I realized that if I liked glasses on women, which I do very much, maybe women would tolerate glasses on me. On naked women glasses work for me the way spike heels or a snake tattoo or an ankle bracelet or a fake beauty spot work for some men—they make the nudity pop out at me; they make the woman seem more naked than she would have seemed if she were completely naked. Also, I want to be very sure that she can see every inch of my richard with utter clarity, and if she is wearing glasses I know that she can if she wants to.

The deciding moment really came when I spent the night with a woman, an office manager, who, I *think* anyway, had sex with me sooner than she wanted to simply to distract me from noticing the fact that her contacts were bothering her. It was very late, but I think she wanted to talk for a while longer, and yet (this is my theory) she hurried to the sex because the extreme intimacy, to her way of thinking, of appearing before me in her glasses was only possible after the less extreme intimacy of fucking me. Several times as we talked I was on the point of saying, since her eyes did look quite unhappily pink, "You want to take out your contacts? I'll take out mine." But I didn't, because I thought it might have a condescending sort of "I know everything about you, baby, your bloodshot eyes give you away" quality. Probably I should have. A few days after that, though, I resumed wearing my glasses to work. My error rate dropped right back down. I was instantly happier. In particular, I recognized the crucial importance of hinges to my pleasure in life. When I open my glasses in the morning before taking a shower and going to work, I am like an excited tourist who has just risen from his hotel bed on the first day of a vacation: I've just flung open a set of double French doors leading out onto a sunlit balcony with a view of the entire whatever—shipping corridor, bay, valley, parking lot. (How can people not like views over motel parking lots in the early morning? The new subtler car colors, the blue-greens and warmer grays, and the sense that all those drivers are leveled in the democracy of sleep and that the glass and hoods out there are cold and even dewy, make for one of the more inspiring visions that life can offer before nine o'clock.) Or maybe French-door hinges are not entirely it. Maybe I think that the hinges of my glasses are a woman's hip sockets: her long graceful legs open and straddle my head all day. I asked Rhody once whether she liked the tickling of my glasses frames on the inside of her thighs. She said, "Usually your glasses are off by then, aren't they?" I admitted that was true. She said she didn't like it when I wore my glasses because she wanted my sense of her open vadge to be more Sisley than Richard Estes. "But I do sometimes like feeling your ears high on my thighs," she conceded. "And if I clamp your ears hard with my thighs I can make more noise without feeling I'm getting out of hand." Rhody was a good, good person, and I probably should not have tried to allude even obliquely to my Fold experiences to her, since she found what little I told her of Fermation repellent; her knowledge of it contributed to our breakup.

Well! I think I have established that there *is* an emotional history to my wearing of glasses. So in saying that she liked them, tall Joyce—who as I sit typing this towers above me now in a state of semi-nudity—was definitely saying the right thing if she was interested in getting to my heart, which she probably wasn't. You have to be extremely careful about complimenting a thirty-five-year-old male temp who has achieved nothing in his life. "Hi, I'm the temp!" That's usually what I say to receptionists on my first day of an assignment; that's the word I use, because it's the word everyone uses, though it was a long time before I stopped thinking that it was a horrible abbreviation, worse than "Frisco." I have been a temp for over ten years, ever since I quit graduate school. The reason I have done nothing with my life is simply that my power to enter the Fold (or "hit the clutch" or "find the Cleft" or "take a personal day" or "instigate an Estoppel") comes and goes. I value the ability, which I suspect is not widespread, but because I don't have it consistently, because it fades without warning and doesn't return until months or years later, I've gotten hooked into a sort of damaging boom-and-bust Kondratieff cycle. When I've lost the power, I simply exist, I do the minimum I have to do to make a living, because I know that in a sense everything I want to accomplish (and I *am* a person with ambitions) is infinitely postponable.

As a rough estimate, I think I have probably spent only a total of two years of personal time in the Fold, if you lump the individual minutes or hours together, maybe even less; but they have been some of the best, most alive times I've had. My life reminds me of the capital-gains tax problem, as I once read about it in an op-ed piece: if legislators keep changing, or even promising to change, the capital-gains percentages, repealing and reinstating the tax, the rational investor will begin to base his investment decisions not on the existing tax laws, but on his certainty of change, which mischannels (the person who wrote the op-ed piece convincingly argued) in some destructive way the circulation of capital. So too with me during those periods when I wait for the return of my ability to stop time: I think, Why should I read Ernest Renan or learn matrix algebra now, since when I'm able to Drop again, I'll be able to spend private hours, or even years, satisfying any fleeting intellectual curiosity while the whole world waits for me? I can always catch up. That's the problem.

People are somewhat puzzled by me when I first show up at their office—What is this unyoung man, this thirty-five-year-old man, doing temping? Maybe he has a criminal past, or maybe he's lost a decade to drugs, or: Maybe He's an Artist? But after a day or two, they adjust, since I am a fairly efficient and good-natured typist, familiar with most of the commonly used kinds of software (and some of the forgotten kinds too, like nroff, Lanier, and NBI, and the good old dedicated DEC systems with the gold key), and I am unusually good at reading difficult handwriting and supplying punctuation for dictators who in their creative excitement forget. Once in a great while I use my Fold-powers to amaze everyone with my apparent typing speed, transcribing a two-hour tape in one hour and that kind of thing. But I'm careful not to amaze too often and become a temp legend, since this is my great secret and I don't want to imperil it—this is the one thing that makes my life worth living. When some of the more intelligent people in a given office ask little prob-ingly polite questions to try to figure me out, I often lie and tell them that I'm a writer. It is almost funny to see how relieved they are to have a way of explaining my lowly work status to themselves. Nor is it so much of a lie, because if I had not wasted so much of my life waiting for the next Fermata-phase to come along I would very likely have writ-ten some sort of a book by now. And I have written a few shorter things.

I'm typing this on a portable electronic typewriter because I don't want to risk putting any of it on the bank's LAN. Local area networks behave erratically in the Fold. When my carpal-tunnel problem gets bad, I use a manual for my private writing; it seems to help. But I don't have to: batter-ies and electricity *do* function in the Fold—in fact, all the laws of physics still obtain, as far as I can tell, but only to the extent that I reawaken them. The best way to describe it is that right now, because I have snapped my fingers, every event everywhere is in a state of gel-like suspension. I can move, and the air molecules part to let me through, but they do it resistingly, reluctantly, and the farther that objects are from me, the more thoroughly they are paused. If someone was riding a motorcycle down a hill before I stopped time "half an hour" ago, the rider will remain motionless on his vehicle unless I walk up to him and give him a push—in which case he will fall down, but somewhat more slowly than if he fell in an unpaused universe. He won't take off down the hill at the speed he was riding, he will just tip over. I used to be tempted to fly small airplanes in the Fold, but I'm not that stupid. Flight, though, is definitely possible, as is the pausing of time on an airplane flight. The world stays halted exactly as it is except where I mess with it, and for the most part I try to be as unobtrusive as possible—as unobtrusive as my lusts let me be. This typewriter, for instance, puts what I type on the page because the act of pressing a letter makes cause and effect function locally. A circuit is completed, a little electricity dribbles from the batteries, etc. I honestly don't know how far outward my personal distortion of the temporary timelessness that I create measurably spreads. I do know that during a Fermata a woman's skin feels soft where it is soft, warm when it is warm—her sweat feels warm when it is warm. It's a sort of reverse Midas touch that I have while in the Fold—the world is inert and statuesque until I touch it and make it live ordinarily.

I had this idea of writing my life story while within a typical chronanistic experience just yesterday. It's almost incredible to think that I've been Dropping since fourth grade and yet I've never made the effort to write about it right while it was going on. I kept an abbreviated log for a while in high school and college—date and time of Drop, what I did, how long in personal minutes or hours or days it took (for a watch usually starts up again in the Fold if I shake it, so I can easily measure how long I have been out), whether I learned anything new or not, and so on. You would think, if a person really could stop the world and get off, as I can, that it would occur to him fairly early on to stop the world in order to record with some care what it felt like to stop the world and get off, for the benefit of the curious. But I now see, even this far into my first autobiographical Fermata, why I never did it before. Sad to say, it is just as hard to write during a Fermation as it is in real time. You still must dole out all the things you have to say one by one, when what you want of course is to say them all at once. But I am going to give it a try. I am thirty-five now, and I have done quite a lot of things, mostly bad, with the Fold's help (including, incidentally, reciting Dylan Thomas's "Poem on His Birthday" apparently from memory at the final session of a class in modern lyric poetry in college: it is a longish poem, and whenever nervousness made me forget a line, I just paused the world by pressing the switch of my Time Perverter—which is what I called the modified garage-door opener that I used in those days—and refreshed my memory by looking at a copy of the text that I had in my notebook, and no one was the wiser)—and if I don't write some of these private adventures down now, I know I'm going to regret it.

Just now I spun around once in my chair in order to surprise myself again with the sight of Joyce's pubic hair. It really is amazing to me that I can do this, even after all these years. She was walking about thirty feet from my desk, across an empty stretch of space, carrying some papers, on her way to someone's cube, and my gaze just launched toward her, diving cleanly, without ripples, through the glasses that she had complimented, taking heart from having to pass through the optical influence of something she had noticed and liked. It was as if I traveled along the arc of my sight and reached her visually. (There is definitely something to those medieval theories of sight that had the eye sending out rays.) And just as my sighted self reached her, she stopped walking for a second, to check something on one of the papers she held, and when she looked down I was struck by the simple fact that today her hair is *braided*.

It is arranged in what I think is called a French braid. Each of the solid clumps of her hair feeds into the overall solidity of the braid, and the whole structure is plaited as part of her head, like a set of glossy external vertebrae. I'm impressed that women are able to arrange this sort of complicated figure, without too many stray strands, without help, in the morning, by feel. Women are much more in touch with the backs of themselves than men are: they can reach higher up on their back, and do so daily to unfasten bras; they can clip and braid their hair; they can keep their rearward blouse-tails smoothly tucked into their skirts. They give thought to how the edges of their underpants look through their pocketless pants from the back. ("Panties" is a word to be avoided, I feel.) But French braids, in which three sporting dolphins dip smoothly under one another and surface in a continuous elegant entrainment, are the most beautiful and impressive results of this sense of dorsal space. As soon as I saw Joyce's braid I knew that it was time to stop time. I needed to feel her solid braid, and her head beneath it, in my palm.

So, just as she started walking again, I snapped my fingers. This is my latest method of entering the Fold, and one of the simpler I have been able to develop (much more straightforward than my earlier mathematical-formula technique, or the sewn calluses, for instance, both of which I will get into later). She didn't hear the snap, only I did—the universe halts at some indeterminate point just before my middle finger swats against the base of my thumb. I got out my Casio typewriter and scooted over here to her on my chair. (I didn't scoot backwards, I scooted frontwards, which isn't easy to do over carpeting, because it is hard to get the proper traction. I wanted to keep my eyes on her.) She was in mid-stride. I reached forward and put my hands on her hipbones. It felt as if there were cashmere or something fancy in the wool, and it was good to feel her hipbones through that soft material, and to see my hands angling to follow the incurve of her waist, which the dress had to an extent hidden. Sometimes when I first touch a woman in the Fold I tense up my arms until they vibrate, so that the shape of whatever is under my palms keeps on being sent through my nerves as new information. I never know exactly what I will do during a Drop. To get her dress out of the way, I lifted its soft hem up over her hips and gathered it into two wingy bunches and tied a big soft knot with them. It had seemed as if she had a tiny potbelly with the dress on (this can be a sexy touch, I think, on some women), but if she had, it disappeared or lost definition as soon as I pulled her panty hose and underpants down as far as I could get them, which wasn't that far because her legs were walkingly apart. (Also, before I pulled down her pantyhose, which is a smoky-blue color, I touched an oval of her skin through a run in the darker part high on her thigh.) And then I was given this sight that I have before me now, of her pubic hair.

I'm not normally a pubic-hair obsessive—I really have no ongoing fetishes, I don't think, because each woman is different, and you never know what particular feature or transition between features is going to grab you and say, "Look at this—you've never thought about exactly this before!"

Each woman inspires her own fetishes. And it isn't that Joyce
has some ludicrous Vagi-fro or massive Koosh-ball explosion
of a sex-goatee—in fact her hair isn't thicker really than most.
It's just that it covers a wider area, maybe, and its blackness
sparkles, if you will—its curving border reaches a little higher
on her stomach. A little?—what am I saying? It's the size of
South America. To think that I could have died and not seen
this—that I could have picked a different temp assignment
when Jenny, my coordinator, told me my choices a few weeks
ago. What is exciting about its extent is maybe that, because
it reaches higher than other women's pubic hair, it becomes
less and more sexual at the same time—the slang for it, like
"pussy hair" and "cunt hair" (I flinch at both those words,
except when I'm close to coming), doesn't apply because it
is no longer, strictly speaking, "pubic" hair at all—its borders are reaching out into soft abdominal love-areas, so love
and sex mix. I wanted to feel it, the dense sisaly lush resilience
of it, which makes that whole hippy part of her body look
extraordinarily graceful. It is a kind of black cocktail dress
under which her clit-heart beats—it has that much *dignity*.

But rather than holding it immediately, I deprived myself
of the sight of it for a little while and instead gently placed
my hand on her braid, which was cool and thick and smooth
and dense, a totally different idea of hair, so different that it
is strange to think of the two orders of hair as sharing the
same word, but which follows the curve of her head in the
same way that her pubic hair follows the curve over her
mound-bone, and when I felt the French-braid sensation
sinking into the hollow of my palm, which craves sexual
shapes and textures, I then went ahead and curled the fingers

of my other hand through her devil's food fur, connecting
the two kinky handfuls of homegrown protein with my
arms, and it felt as if I were hot-wiring a car; my heart's twin
carburetors roared into life. That's all I did, then I started typing this before I forgot the feeling. Maybe that's all I will do.
That sexy, *sexy* pubic hair! I'm noticing now that its contours
are similar to those of a black bicycle seat: a black leather seat
on a racing bicycle. Maybe this is why those sad sniffers of
comic legend sniff girls' bicycle seats? No, for them it isn't
the shape, it's the fact that the seat has been between a girl's
legs. They are truly pathetic. I have no sympathy to spare for
compulsions other than my own. I would, though, like to
rescue the correspondence between pubic hair and narrow
black-leather bicycle seats from them.

All right, I think that is enough for now. I've been in the
Fold for, let's see, almost four hours and written eight single-
spaced pages, and the problem is that if I stay in too long
I'll have jet lag tomorrow, since according to my inner clock
it will be four hours later than it is. Usually I don't spend
nearly this long in a Drop. I am going to put Joyce's clothes
back in order and smooth out her dress (I would never have
tied a knot in it if she wore a cotton dress, because the wrin-
kles would show up too much and puzzle her) and I'm going
to scoot back to my desk and finish out the day. The good
thing is that if she brings me a tape to do later this afternoon, I will be much more relaxed and therefore likable
than if I hadn't partially stripped her without her knowledge
or consent. I will jest knowingly and winningly with her. I
will compliment her on today's scarf—which isn't, honestly,
quite as nice as the Cyrillic one. (Maybe when she was get-

ting dressed this morning she put on this knit dress and then remembered that I had admired her scarf, and maybe she thought that wearing it again as well would be too direct a Yes from her; but then again maybe the reason she was wearing the dress this soon again was that she had liked my complimenting her on her scarf and wanted to allude to that compliment indirectly by wearing the same dress with another scarf.) This new one is a Liberty pattern of purply grays and greens, definitely worth smiling at and even acknowledging outright. But I don't want to get into one of those awful running-compliment patterns, where I have to mention her scarves every time she wears one.

The other thing I should say is that under normal circumstances I would probably give serious thought to "poaching an egg" at this point, but because I have written all this, and because this is, I believe, going to be the very beginning of a sort of autobiography, I can't. What a surprise, though, to find this Casio typewriter acting as chaperon! (Maybe what I will do is go ahead, but not mention it.)

Has anyone yet said publicly how nice it is to write on rubber with a ballpoint pen? The slow, fat, ink-rich line, rolled over a surface at once dense and yielding, makes for a multidimensional experience no single sheet of paper can offer. Right now dozens of Americans are making repetitive scrolly designs on the soft white door-seals of their refrigerators, or they are directing their pens around the layered side-steppes and toe-bulbs of their sneakers (heads bent, as elders give them advice), or they are marking shiny initials on one of those gigantic, dumb, benevolent erasers (which always bounce in unforeseen directions when dropped, and seem so selfless, so apolitical, so completely uninterested in doing anything besides erasing large mistakes for which they were not responsible), and then using the eraser to print these same initials several times, backward, on a knee or forearm, in a fading progression. These are rare pleasures.

And then someone mentions several kinds of rubber penmanship in his opening paragraph. Has a useful service been performed? A few readers, remembering that they did once enjoy taking down a toll-free phone number on the blade of a clean Rubbermaid spatula, react with guarded agreement: "Yes, I guess I am one of those not-so-uncommon people who have had that sort of rare experience." Infrequent events in the lives of total strangers are now linked; but the pleasure itself is too fragile, too incidental, to survive such forced affiliation undamaged. Regrettably, multiplying the idea of a thing's rarity is nearly identical in effect to multiplying the thing itself: its rarity departs. Some readers may never again engage so unthinkingly in this particular strain of idleness. It is no more common than it was before I brought it up, but it is more commonplace.

Rarity, then, is an emotion as much as it is a statistical truth. Just say the word over to yourself: *Rare. O rarer than rare.* A long, piercing curve of light appears and fades in one's darkened memory. It's like that diminishing cry of cartoon characters when they are tricked into running off a cliff. *The rare book room. A rare disease. Rarefied air. A miracle of rare device.* Comprehended in the notion are all sorts of contributory pangs: brevity, chances barely missed, awe, the passing of great men and glorious eras. Frequency is a sudden movement of many wings, a riffle through a worn paperback; rarity holds the single hushing index finger raised. And yet the absolute number of "raremes" is enormous—too large, in fact, for us to give each one of them the rapt monocular attention it deserves. Not only are there priceless misstamped nickels, oddball aurora borealises hanging their ball gowns over unpopulated areas, fraternal bananas enclosed in a single skin, holes-in-one, and authentic Georges de la Tours; there are also all the varied sorts of human talent and permutations of character: the master mimic of frog sounds, the memory prodigy, the man who can mix wit with sympathy. The universe of rares is surprisingly crowded, and yet it is somehow capable of holding its inmates in seeming isolation, each of them floating in a radiantly placental, fluid-filled sphere of amazement, miles from any neighbor.

By there is ferment, too, in this universe. The turnover rate is very high. One disc jockey, in a fit of inspiration, will substitute *colder in the shrubs* for *colder in the suburbs*, or *T-storms* for *thunderstorms*; within two weeks every keen-eared DJ in the country is in step, and these phrases, cooling quickly, are soon remaindered to lesser microphones. Forgotten commonplaces rare up their heads, and soiled rarities are tossed back into the commonplace, twenty-four hours a day, in processes as inevitable as the cycles of rain and evaporation. But in this churning lies our perplexity. Since rarity constitutes part of the pleasure we take in many of the things we value, how rare should we allow a rareme to remain when it is in our power to influence its frequency?

Maybe good ideas should supplant bad ones without the resistance of prejudice or habit; maybe inside information should become public knowledge with the shortest possible delay. We act as if it should. Automatic mechanisms are in place for the efficient display of any hidden gem—a clever household hint, a new theory, a patent, a fairly good poem. Seed money is everywhere. Venture capitalists, those sleepless invigilators, roam the laboratories for the tiniest tremor of a possibility, force-feed it ten million dollars, pump it up, bring it public, and move on. Grant committees and arts competitions chew through the applicant pools, funding anything that moves. Contrarians trample one another to buy unfashionable stocks. "New and Noteworthy" columns take any gruntling of an innovation and give it a paragraph, a title with a pun in it, and a close-cropped picture. We are chastened by past mistakes: Mendel died ignored; Brahms was hissed; Harvey's patients dropped him when he came out with *The Circulation of the Blood*. This kind of embarrassment must not happen in our lifetime!

At times it's fun to be part of a society so intent on institutionalizing its response to novelty. Our toes are curled right around the leading edge of the surfboard. Nothing far out will catch *us* off guard. We will monitor left field continually, and no hint of activity from that quarter will elude our scrutiny.

But there are ill effects, nervous tics, symptoms of exhaustion, that arise in an audience when it oversolicits the heteroclite. Newness ought to suffer a period of frost—it should even have to submit, for its own good, to entrenched and outraged resistance. Neglect gives a winsome oddity more time to perform important tests on itself; widespread narrow-mindedness shelters surprise. No one will blame a publisher who has discovered an out-of-print minor masterpiece and feels it his duty to enrich and uplift the human spirit by publishing it in paperback, with a beautiful, spare, up-to-the-minute cover design. That is his job. But sometimes we can't help wishing he would wait, and just buy one old copy for himself from an antiquarian dealer, preserving for at least a few more years the delight of private, proprietary knowledge, the ecstasy of arriving at something underappreciated at the end of a briareous ramification of footnotes, since the hope of such secrets is one of the things that keep us reading.

Rough timetables, "appreciation schedules," may be of some guidance. That pad dotted on both sides with suction cups, to which you can vertically affix a wet bar of soap while you are in the shower? It should remain unmentioned by any magazine's "New and Noteworthy" column for six months. Each of us should have a fair chance of finding it, hanging unheralded from a hook in the hardware store, on our own. A good poem, as Horace suggested, ought to have a nine-year news blackout. And a major leisure item—a new sort of inflatable raft, for example—deserves at least five summers of quiet superiority before it gets a Best Buy rating from *Consumer Reports* and leans against the wall in the sporting-goods department at the high-volume discounters. After all, this successful raft—with its revolutionary osmotic inflater-valve—displaces several other very good makes of raft, which once so proudly rode the crest; and when we look through the still-hopeful catalogs of these inferior raft-crafters, and sense their anguish, deepening monthly, as they watch their sales go into steep decline, then *they* begin to take on rarity—the rarity of the underdog, one of the most seductive kinds—and we discover ourselves feeling, too soon, that we must root for the second-rate product. (Haven't you felt a peculiar sort of worry about the chair in your living room that no one sits in? Haven't you sometimes felt sleeve-tugs of compassion and guilt over an article of clothing that you dislike and therefore scarcely wear? Haven't you at least once secretly sat down in the hardly-sat-in chair, wearing that ugly shirt, in order to rectify these inequities?) A little lengthening of the time it takes for new merit to out, for rare proficiencies to make their sudden bundle, would allow our sympathy for the underdog and our excitement in superiority to coincide; too rapid a transmittal of the knowledge of relative greatness, on the other hand, eliminates that beautiful period when these emotions overlap.

Subtotaling, then, we note that civilization ought to be superficially pigheaded, suspicious of all subversion, so that rarity can leap in with her accordion and startle the anatomy lesson. If the sadly underrated is kept sadly underrated, righteousness and a sense of urgent mission stay on the side of the deserving. But when all the goodies are pincered the moment they surface, when zoning rules demand public art in exchange for additional floor space, when writers curtail their finer efforts because the merest suggestion of expertise is enough to coast on for a decade, then one is unwillingly forced, on behalf of originality itself, to defend authority, stringency, unbendingness—not things one defends with real moral relish. So let the rare stay rare, at least for a while. Every piece of bad design praised does its bit to keep good designs under wraps. We need many incompetent arbiters; we need more choices to be foolish and uninformed.

Some desert fathers have gotten carried away, though. Say you are a genius, and you have just done something that has never been done before. There it lies, on your legal pad or your patio, as rare as it could possibly be. In a week or a year it might glint in thousands of other minds, like the tiny repeating images in a beetle's eye. Paul Valéry has some stern words for you: "Every mind considered powerful begins with the fault that makes it known," he writes. And: "the strongest heads, the most sagacious inventors, the most exacting connoisseurs of thought, must be unknown men, misers, who die without giving up their secret." Even putting an idea in words, according to Arthur Schopenhauer, is a sellout: "As soon as our thinking has found words it ceases to be sincere or at bottom serious. When it begins to exist for others it ceases to live in us." The self-canceling quality of these verbal arguments for silence is obvious. Still, if behind them is simply the wish for a kind of privacy, for the insulation of inattention, for a few delays in the final sentencing of a thought, for a little sorrow intermixed with one's eager self-expression, then any prudent introvert would raise a concurring absinthe glass.

Things often work better, too, when the portions of each person's life that are wholly devoted to a quest for the rare are themselves somewhat infrequent. The staggering fluke and the exhilarating pathology ought to surprise their first discoverers as much as they surprise the rest of us. It is always more pleasing when the sweepstakes is won by the family who sent off their entry distractedly, in the midst of errands and trips to the vet, than when it is won by that man with the flat voice, in the hooded parka, who sent in five hundred thirty-seven separate entries—except that ultimately rarity accrues to him as well, once we contemplate him: all those unshaven mornings at the post office, those readings of the fine-print contest guidelines, those copyings of "Dove is One Quarter Cleansing Cream" on three-by-five pieces of paper.

For everyone besides that rare man in the parka, the provisional moral may be: Pursue truth, not rarity. The atypical can fend for itself: our innate, unconquerable human appetite for it will never let it lie low for long. And very often, when we are looking over several common truths, holding them next to one another in an effort to feel again what makes them true, rarities will mysteriously germinate in the charged spaces between them, like those lovely, ghostly zings that a guitarist's fingers make, as they clutch from chord to chord.

(1984)

THE PROJECTOR

The finest moment in *The Blob* (1958) occurs in a small-town movie theater, during a showing of something called *Daughter of Horror*. While the pre-McLuhanite projectionist reads his hardcover book, the Blob—a giant protean douche-bag—begins to urge its heat-seeking toxic viscosity through ten tiny slits in an air vent. Past the turning movie reel, we watch the doomed projectionist glance out the viewport at the screen, preparing for a "changeover"—an uninterrupted switch from the running projector, whose twenty-minute reel is almost over, to the second, idle one, which is all threaded and ready to roll. He senses something at his back; he turns; he gives the flume of coalesced protoplasm a level look—then it gets him. Now unattended, the first projector plays past the cue for the changeover and runs out of film. The disgruntled audience looks around and spots the Blob (in an image that must have inspired the development of the Play-Doh Fun Factory) extruding itself in triumph from all four of the little windows—two projector ports and two viewports—in the theater's rear wall.

Chuck Russell's remake of *The Blob* (1988) brings every

detail, or almost every detail, of the first film neatly up to date. The movie-within-a-movie is now entitled *Garden Tool Massacre*. "Isn't it awfully late to be trimming the hedges?" a camp counselor mutters while making out with his girlfriend, having noticed a masked stranger at work on the shrubbery after dark. "Wait a minute," he then says, suspicions aroused. "Hockey season ended months ago." Cut to the booth, where "Hobbs," the bored projectionist (whose life will indeed prove to be "solitary, poor, nasty, brutish, and short"), his head again seen past a turning reel of film, reads a magazine and fiddles left-handedly with a yo-yo. The second-generation Blob, far peppier and more enterprising than its forebear, pukes its way briskly up the air-conditioning duct and plasters the unhappy Hobbs to the ceiling. Moments later, the manager, looking up, discovers his colleague, a Ralph Steadman grimace on his face, half consumed in an agony of Handi-Wrap and dyed cornstarch, the yo-yo still rising and falling from his twitching finger.

Why the addition of the yo-yo? the student of film technology may wonder. Is it merely a gratuitous prop, or does it tell us something? I suspect that the yo-yo is a reference to the classical principle of the movie reel, which repeatedly rewinds and relinquishes its length of film. The reason Mr. Russell had the iconography of the movie reel very much on his mind in shooting this scene, I think, is that, despite all his diligent updating of cultural references, and despite the elaborate verisimilitude of the movie's gruesomeness, he was not quite able to bring himself to reveal to us the reality of modern theatrical-movie projection. For the terrifying reality is that *film is no longer projected from reels.*

Fig. 1. *On the top platter (1) film unfurls from the inside out, and winds up on the middle platter (2). The lowest platter (3) is a spare, used for a second feature. The canted console (4), containing the xenon lamphouse and sound equipment, aims the image from the projector (5) through the glass projector port (6), and onto the screen. In the soundhead (7), a solar cell interprets the soundtrack. The projectionist keeps an eye on image quality through the viewport (8).*

Film is projected from platters. The platter system (Fig. 1), first invented by a German projectionist, Willie Burth, and perfected by Norelco, in the Netherlands, about twenty years ago, works this way: The film arrives from the distributor on five or six reels in an octagonal steel suitcase. The projectionist splices the film from these reels together, winding it in one big spiral onto one of (typically) three horizontal circular steel disks, each roughly four feet in diameter. When the projectionist wants to set up a show, he pulls the beginning of the film from the middle of the platter, threads it through the platter's central "brain" (its lumpily massed rollers look somewhat cerebral), thence around a few guide rollers screwed into the wall or the ceiling, and loads it into the sprockets of the projector. After it passes through the "gate" (where it is actually projected), the film usually travels through the sound head (where a light reads the optical soundtrack), loops around several more guide rollers, and ends up being wound in another huge spiral on one of the other horizontal platters. Because the film leaves from the middle of the platter, instead of the outside, rewinding between shows, reel by reel, is no longer necessary. And each theater needs only one projector per screen, rather than the traditional tagteam alternating two.

There are a few revival houses in Los Angeles and New York that continue to show films on two projectors from reels, but the vast majority of the country's theaters—art houses and mall-plexes alike—currently employ the platter system, and have for the past decade. Yet of the projector-movies from this period that I have seen (movies that include a moment or two in a contemporary projection booth, I mean), not one—not Chuck Russell's *Blob* or Joe Dante's *Gremlins* (1984: gremlins invade theater and play Reel 4 of *Snow White*), or *Night of the Comet* (1984: couple spend night in steel-firewalled projection booth and escape being turned into red dust or killer maniacs by comet), not Susan Seidelman's wonderful *Desperately Seeking Susan* (1985: we'll get to this one later) or *Gas, Food, Lodging* (1992: girl falls for Chicano projectionist)—dares give us a glimpse of a turning platter. I was sure, having read a description (in Carol J. Clover's thoughtful book *Men, Women, and Chain Saws: Gender in the Modern Horror Film*) of a despicable Italian zombie movie called *Demons* (1985), that, because its action—fountains of pus and helicopter-blade disembowelings—is set within a fully automated and (of course) transcendently evil movie theater, with an unmanned projection booth, and because the second-largest manufacturer of movie projectors in the world happens to be Milan's Cinemeccanica, that at least here, in this admittedly unsavory setting, we would be shown something approaching the technical truth about movie projection. But no: although the demonic equipment blinks with a few more lights than usual, it is fitted with the familiar pairs of reels up front.

These lapses of realism probably have more to do with iconographic inertia than with any sort of conspiracy or coverup on the part of movie people. It isn't that "they" don't want us to know that the friendly century-old reel of celluloid, the reel that has fueled a million puns and that more than any other image means movies to us, has been superseded by a separate triple-tiered mechanism that, while full of visual interest, and quite beautiful in its indolent, wedding-cake-on-display sort of way, is less intuitively comprehensible than its predecessor. Hollywood producers don't care whether we are aware that the platter system reduced the participatory role of the projectionist and helped make the multiplex theater financially attractive. (The eighteen-screen Cineplex Odeon in Los Angeles, for example, requires only two projectionists at any one time, and the twenty-six-screen complex in Brussels is comfortably tended by eight.) Nor do they care whether or not we know that platter hardware is, according to some critics, rougher on a movie print than reel-to-reel projection was.

"The platter is death to film," Dr. Jan-Christopher Horak, the senior curator of films at the George Eastman House, in Rochester, told me. A print now must twist a hundred and eighty degrees on its axis as it completes the large open-air loop that leads from the feed platter through the projector to the takeup platter; this subjects it, Horak says, to a kind of helical stress that film stock has not previously had to withstand. He has been finding "strange stretch marks that aren't vertical, as you might expect, but horizontal" on platter-fed films. And the platter system, he says, allows for unattended operation: if a hardy chunk of filth gets caught in the gate of the projector, it can scratch the film for hundreds of feet unremedied. Horak also mentions the lost-frame problem: every time a projectionist "builds" a feature on a platter, he must cut the leaders off each component reel and splice the ends in place; then, when the film is "broken down" at the end of its run, those splices are cut and the leaders reattached for shipping. In the process, each reel loses at least a frame of film. The more theaters a film visits, the shorter it gets.

Dick Twichell—a wise and careful projectionist at a twelve-screen Loew's Theatre complex in greater Rochester, not far from Horak's archival collection—admits that ambient dirt can cause serious trouble now. "Static electricity becomes more of a problem, because the film is out in the open air and attracts dust," he says. The guide rollers, often made of plastic rather than metal, contribute to, rather than dissipate, static. And when a plex theater does something called "interlocking"— the simultaneous running of a single print through two or even three separate projectors, aimed at different screens— the film can travel hundreds of feet over guide rollers, paying out along the ceiling and returning low, inches from the floor, drawing dust along the way.

On the other hand, Twichell disagrees that the round trip to and from the platter physically overstresses a print. "If that were true, the splices would come apart, and they almost never do," he says. In fact, Twichell, like many in the film industry, is of the opinion that platter hardware is far gentler on prints than reels were. A takeup reel had a primitive clutch: it pulled the film forcibly off the teeth of the projector's lower sprocket, wearing out its perforations: a print would last perhaps three hundred runs, certainly no more than seven hundred, before becoming flimsy and easily torn. Now, on platters, a print can run almost indefinitely without sustaining that sort of mechanical damage. (There is a platter disaster known as a "brain-wrap," but it is relatively rare.) Disney routinely gets ten or twenty thousand showings from a single print in its theme parks; often the dyes in the emulsion fade before the film succumbs.

Constant rewinding, which platters eliminate, was itself a major source of harm. "Fully nine-tenths of the damage to film comes from the process known as 'pulling down' in rewinding," says the 1912 *Motion Picture Handbook*. The rainmarks, as they are called, that distance us from an old Buster Keaton picture, say, were probably made while it was being rewound, not while it was being cranked through the projector. Projectionists were traditionally tinkerers, techies, taciturn isolates with dirty fingernails; of necessity they worked (and still do work, some of them) surrounded by grease pots, oilcans, dirty rags, swapped-out components, and (before xenon bulbs came in, in the sixties) by the stubs of spent carbons from the carbon-arc lamps, each of which lasted no more than half an hour. Chuck McCann, who plausibly plays the hefty, chain-smoking hero of a 1970 film called *The Projectionist* (which is a sort of remake of the 1924 Buster Keaton movie *Sherlock, Junior*: the one about a projectionist who, dozing off on a stool by one of his machines, dreams that he has entered the film that he is showing), gets angry at Rodney Dangerfield (the manager) and slams a reel of film onto the rewinder, cranking hard and maintaining tension by resting his palm on the reel. The more brute film handling—rewinding, threading, splicing—that the typical projectionist was forced to do, the more beat-up the film became.

The Projectionist is filled with fun snippets from old movies, as is *Cinema Paradiso* (1989), a horribly sentimental Italian creation that is nonetheless accurate in portraying the local projectionist, rather than any director or studio head, as the person with the final cut. *Cinema Paradiso*'s previewing priest rings a bell anytime people kiss onscreen, and the projectionist dutifully marks the moment in the reel with a strip of paper so that he can remove the kiss later. In truth, though, projectionists, at least in the United States, were more likely to be furtive editors and clip-collectors on their own (as the creators of *The Projectionist* seemingly were) than on behalf of local censors: they would simply cut out a few feet, or a frame or two, of an image or a sequence they liked. Commonly, they collected "favorite movie stars, and especially scenes or shots that had pieces of female anatomy in them," Horak told me; the Eastman House now owns some of these collections. One projectionist told me that if you cut two frames from a scene where a camera is dollied sidewise, and you then view these frames through a stereoscope, you can simulate 3-D. After years in the projection business, this man has lost all interest in watching movies, and he has canceled HBO and Cinemax, but he continues to accumulate 3-D frames. He cuts them out, he hastened to say, only if they appear in a trailer, or at the front or back of a reel, where frames are meant to be lost anyway. Other projectionists may be less ethical. It could well be that hands-off platter automation helps projectionists resist the powerful temptation to keep souvenirs from the films that pass through their theaters.

Even with automation, though, there is a fair amount of under-the-hood maintenance connected with tending a projector. Early in *The Inner Circle* (1991), Tom Hulce, who plays Stalin's projectionist, plucks something from his shirt pocket.

"What's that you're poking in the projector?" asks the alarmed KGB official.

"Toothbrush," Hulce says. "Very convenient for cleaning. I always carry one with me."

The KGB man studies it, sniffs it. "The old projectionist never had anything like that," he says, impressed.

Recently, after the last show of the night of *The Remains of the Day*, I watched Stephan Shelley, senior projectionist at the Grand Lake Theatre, in Oakland, California, clean the vitals of one of his eight projectors with a pale-blue Colgate toothbrush. ("A clean, used toothbrush is ideal," advises the user's manual for the current Century MSC-TA 35-mm projector with self-turning lens turret.) Shelley greases the rods and gears of his Century projectors every morning; he uses rubbing alcohol and Q-Tips on the equipment daily as well; and he keeps a vigilant eye on the level of the oil bath in the all-important intermittent movement. (Seventy-millimeter film, he says, which has a magnetic rather than an optical soundtrack, leaves a projector especially dirty, because ferrous particles from the magnetic strip come off in the machine.) Fully cross-trained, he also fixes popcorn poppers when they break. There are occasional reports of projectionists less knowledgeable than Shelley who, having run out of projector oil, resort in desperation to pouring popcorn butter in the machines to keep them from freezing up. This practice voids the warranty, however.

Besides platters, the other notable recent development in projectorware is the aforementioned xenon bulb, a two-thousand-watt, foot-long, thousand-dollar item that illuminates a film by sending eighty amperes of direct current through a quartz envelope containing ten atmospheres of excitable xenon. It makes a B-movie sort of zap when it comes on. Through a tiny green portal in the lamphouse, you can peer in on it and watch it radiating away, cooled by indefatigable fans. It, too, caused a flutter of dissent when first introduced: charged xenon was said to produce a noticeably harsher, bluer light than the glowing carbon tips of the arc lamp did. Also, bulbs occasionally "fail violently" (i.e., explode), damaging the focusing mirror in the lamphouse. But the arc lamp gave off toxic fumes, and it was moody: movies were especially luminous on windy days, when the exhaust chimneys drew better and the carbons consequently burned brighter. Objections to xenon have pretty much died down; the only legitimate gripe the moviegoer can make now is that when a bulb fails, even nonviolently (this usually happens after about two thousand hours of service), it takes a while to alert someone in the theater and get the projector stopped, and, since platters can't be reversed, the audience will miss the stretch of the movie that ran with sound and no picture.

We now know more of the projector's earliest history, thanks to Christopher Rawlence's recent book *The Missing Reel: The Untold Story of the Lost Inventor of Moving Pictures*. It was the movie projector, not the movie camera, that gave early visionaries trouble, since the projector must hold each frame still longer, and must snap to the next frame faster, than a camera does when it exposes film. The original invention, defined as an affair of toothed sprockets that engage with a flexible perforated band carrying sequential images, probably ought to be attributed to Louis Aimé Augustin Le Prince (1841–1890?), a ceramicist and enameler who worked in Leeds. Le Prince filed the relevant patent in 1886 but disappeared several years later, days before he was to leave for the United States with a crated demo model of his epochal "deliverer." That Thomas Edison's lawyers had him killed, Rawlence suggests, is unclear.

Edison, tireless and shrewd in his appropriation of other people's work, unsurprisingly claimed sole authorship of the "Vitascope," but he and his projector-development team had done little more than slap the Wizard's name on a machine actually built by Thomas Armat, a Washington inventor, which incorporated principles conceived by Le Prince. Armat's historic hand was working the crank when, on April 23, 1896, the screen at Koster & Bial's Music Hall, on West Thirty-fourth Street, wowed journalists with the

"Perfect Reproduction of Noted Feminine Figures and Their Every Movement."

Early projectionists in the wake of Armat were inventors and repairmen, but they were also performers, interpreting the emotional tone of a film by varying the film speed. "The really high-class operator, who produces high-class work on the screen, must and will vary his speed to suit the subject being projected," F. H. Richardson's 1912 textbook advised. For example:

[A]s a rule solemn scenes will be improved if the machine turns slowly. Take, for instance . . . the Pathé Passion Play; probably the Bible patriarchs in real life actually moved as fast as anyone else. They may have, upon occasion, even run. Nevertheless rapid action does not suit our preconceived notions of such things. I have often seen the Pathé Passion Play run at such enormous speed that the characters were jumping around the screen like a lot of school boys. Such an exhibition was disgusting to the audience and offensive to those of deeply religious inclination and who revere those characters.

Even after the electric motor eased the physical labor of the projectionist, silent film studios often furnished cue sheets along with their prints, which itemized the changes in speed that, like tempo markings on a piano score, were an important part of the experience of films such as *The Birth of a Nation*. One of the reasons silent movies can seem so ridiculous now (in addition to the fact that some of them *are* ridiculous, of course) is that they are frequently presented at the

fixed, twenty-four-frames-per-second rate adopted for equipment in the late 1920s, in conjunction with the optical soundtrack (the ear can't tolerate changes in speed the way the eye
can), rather than at variable rates more in the vicinity of sixteen frames a second, as was conventional until then.

But despite these momentous changes—the stabilization
of film speed; sound; Technicolor; the replacement of nitrate-
based film with fire-retardant acetate; xenon bulbs; platteri-
zation—the really remarkable thing about the evolution of
the projector over the past century is how similar in motive
essentials a 1994 Simplex machine is to the original Armat/
Le Prince design. Film still moves on sprockets with sixteen
teeth, and the crucial "intermittent" sprocket—the one that
actually stops and starts the film—is still powered, as it was
at Koster & Bial's Music Hall, by a lovely piece of precision
machinery called the Geneva movement, which was first
developed by Swiss watchmakers to prevent springs from
being overwound. The Geneva movement has two main
pieces: a Maltese cross (or star, or starwheel) and a more pedestrian cam, both of which splash around half submerged in
oil. The pin on the steadily turning cam slips into the slot in
the Maltese cross and forces it to rotate a quarter of a turn
and then stop dead, immobilized by the cam's circular edge.
When the star is stopped, a single immobile image floods the
theater screen for a few hundredths of a second; when it turns,
the film advances under cover of shuttered darkness. The
moviegoer's brain, hoodwinked by this succession of still
lives, obligingly infers motion.

"You know what a Maltese cross is?" an itinerant projector-
repairman with questionable toilet habits asks an incompe-

Fig. 2. *The cams turns (1) until the pin engages the Maltese cross (2), giving it a quarter turn and pulling the film down one frame (3). At (4), the pin releases the cross.*

tent projectionist near the end of Wim Wenders's mammoth film-fleuve, *Kings of the Road*. The projectionist takes a guess: Some kind of drink? The repairman shakes his head sadly and tries to explain it to him. "Without this little thing, there'd be no film industry!" he says. The projectionist is unimpressed, and (because *Kings of the Road* is a semi-comprehensible art movie) he casually inhales the flame from a cigarette lighter to close out the scene. But the workings of the true star system, though they may take a moment to grasp (Fig. 2), repay meditation: seldom has a mechanism so simple, so unexpectedly heraldic, persisted without modification at the center of a ruthless business that has otherwise undergone continuous technical, artistic, and financial upheavals.

The Simplex projector, which many hold to be the finest, is built in Omaha by a company called Ballantyne, which also makes theatrical spotlights and high-tech chicken cookers. The Maltese cross *within* the Simplex projector, however, is manufactured in Glendale Heights, Illinois, the work of a privately held company called La Vezzi Precision Incorporated, run by fifty-one-year-old Al La Vezzi. Al La Vezzi's grandfather, Edward La Vezzi, got his start, during the First World War, by milling the worn teeth off projector sprockets and sweating new brass ones on. Now, in a sort of benevolent monopoly, La Vezzi's company makes sprockets and intermittent movements for Simplex, Century, and Ballantyne projectors (all three brands are co-owned, and based in Omaha), and also for several companies in Europe and Asia, and for Christie projectors made in Cypress, California. For Christie, La Vezzi developed a sealed, belt-driven intermittent movement, called the Ultramittent, that never needs oiling. La Vezzi Precision is also responsible for the legendary VKF sprocket—the Very Kind to Film sprocket, that is— whose teeth are smoothed in meaningful ways by computer-controlled four-axis machining centers. The manufacture of the VKF sprocket is a "no-brainer," however, according to Mr. La Vezzi, compared to making the Maltese cross, where serious flaws are measured in millionths of an inch. "The slot of a star has to be perfect," he says, pronouncing "perfect" with inspiring plosiveness.

Will there always be intermittent sprockets, and the projectors they serve, at work in the world? Will later generations of movie watchers know how similar a projector sounds to an idling VW Beetle? Will they, when viewing that superb early scene in Charlie Chaplin's *Modern Times*, realize that, though Chaplin is ostensibly dragged down into the bowels of a huge "Electro Steel Corp." machine, he is really miming a piece of flexible film and threading himself through the sprockets of a movie projector? I've watched quite a few projector-movies recently (including one that I haven't been able to splice in anywhere here, called *The Smallest Show on Earth*, in which Peter Sellers plays an old projectionist who disrupts a Western when he gets drunk in the booth), but I watched every one of them on videotape. I paused, rewound, fast-forwarded, played, and paused again so much in studying the last scene of *Desperately Seeking Susan*, for instance (Aidan Quinn kisses Rosanna Arquette against a Simplex projector playing a sci-fi movie about mutant attackers— Rosanna's back arrests the winged chariot of the movie reel and the film frame melts on the screen), that the black plastic housing of the rented video gave off an unusually strong and pleasing smell of miniature VCR servomotors and hot printed-circuit boards when I at last, having subjected the lovers' frame-melting embrace to a level of scrutiny it was never meant to bear, ejected it.

But that single 35-mm rectangle of color film contains, it is estimated, the equivalent of forty megabytes of digital information: forty megabytes, the contents of an entire small hard disk, in *every frame* of a movie. Even if one assumes all sorts of clever data compression, it is difficult to imagine digital storage systems matching the Van Eyckian resolution of the chemical grains on a strip of 35– or 70–mm movie film anytime soon. Projectors, and the durably whirling Maltese crosses inside them, may still be around when, in another thirty years, a third, magnificently reimagined *Blob* oozes into the projection area of the local eight-plex and begins stirring up trouble. And by then, perhaps, horror-film makers will be brave enough to show us a few platters.

(1994)

LEADING WITH THE GRUMPER

This[1] may be the funniest and best-smelling work of profound lexicographical slang-scholarship ever published. Some may respect the hint of Elmer's glue in recent printings of Partridge's *Dictionary of Slang and Unconventional English (8th ed.)*, or the faint traces of burlap and cocoa bean that linger deep in *The Oxford Dictionary of Modern Slang*, or even the fume of indoor swimming pool that clings to the paperbound decolletage of *Slang!: The Topic-By-Topic Dictionary of Contemporary American Lingoes*. But a single deep draught of J. E. Lighter's magnificent *Historical Dictionary of American Slang (Volume I, A-G)* is a higher order of experience: it smells like a high-ceilinged bare room freshly painted white—clean and sunlit, full of reverberative promise and proud of its mitered corners, although with a mildly intoxicating or hyperventilational "finish." Since these one thousand and six pages embrace more concentrated filth, vilification, and depravity than any contiguously printed sequence is likely to contain until Lighter's Volume II (H-R) appears in the spring of 1996,

[1] *Historical Dictionary of American Slang (Volume 1, A–G)*, edited by J. E. Lighter.

we may momentarily question the appropriateness of so guile-less a fragrance. Yet reading onward (and Lighter really must be read, or at least deeply browsed, rather than consulted—the book belongs on every patriotic coffee table) we begin to acknowledge its aptness, for this work makes us see American slang—a dingy, stuffy, cramped apartment that we've lived in for so long now that it bores and irritates us—with sudden latex-based clarity and awe. What a spacious, cheery gallery we now have in which to tour our swearwords! How delightfully chronological and typographically tasteful it all is! How firmly principled, how unchaotic, how waltzable-in!

And mainly, how unexpectedly funny. To judge by his helpful introduction, Mr. Lighter, who has been laboring on this project for twenty-five years, is not himself a wildly comic person, but he is an exact and deliberate and histori-cally minded person, and he has a rare ability for positioning formerly funny words and phrases in settings that allow them to become funny once more. He is slang's great straight man. I never suspected that I would again laugh aloud at the phrase "broken-dick motherfucker," having found it inert for some time—but no, reading (on the plane) one of the several citations under "**broke-dick** *adj.* worthless.—usu. considered vulgar," I was suddenly, mystifyingly, pounding the tray-table. So too with the entry for *airhole*:

airhole *n.* [partly euphem.] ASSHOLE, 1 & 2.
a1925 in Fauset *Folklore from N.S.* 134: Mary had a little lamb,/Its face was black as charcoal,/Every time it shook its tail,/He showed his little airhole.

1985 *Webster* (ABC-TV): I wear socks with black shoes. A lot of people think I'm an airhole.

And *fern*:

fern *n. Stu.* the buttocks. *Joc.*
1965 N.Y.C. high-school student: How's your fern [after a fall]?
1965 Adler *Vietnam Letters* 99: You know, the hardest part of all this is the feeling of sitting around on our ferns, doing nothing.

And even:

asshole *n.* [ME *arce-hoole*] Also (*Rare* in U.S.) **arsehole.**— usu. considered vulgar. [See note at ASS, *n.*, which is usually considered to be less offensive. Additional phrases in which these words appear interchangeably may be found at ASS.]
1. the anus or rectum [. . . .]
1987 D. Sherman *Main Force* 183: when I tell you to do something, I expect to hear your asshole pop, do you understand me?

You enter, while studying this book, the west wing of verbal consciousness—the realm of *slangfarbenmelodie*, of alliterative near-similarity and drunken lateralism and chiming hostility purged of its face-to-face context and abstracted into music: you are in the presence, at times, of the only good things that a million anonymous bullies and sadistic drill-sergeants and cruel-minded, mean-spirited frat boys or sorority girls have bequeathed to the world:

> **chicken-fucker** n. a depraved or disgusting fellow.—usu. constr. with *baldheaded*.—usu. considered vulgar.
>
> **1953** in Legman *Rationale* 20: Suddenly two bald-headed men enter, and the parrot says, "You two chicken-fuckers come out in the henhouse with me." **1976–79** Duncan & Moore *Green Side Out* 276 [ref. to *ca*1960]: All right ya bald-headed chicken-fuckers, I want this area policed the fuck up. **1967–80** McAleer & Dickson *Unit Pride* 287 [ref. to Korean War]: Heave in the first shovelful . . . and run like a baldheaded chicken-fucker.

Of course, nice, gentle people invent slang, too, once in a while. And nice, gentle people can take private satisfaction in slang that they would never more than mutter. In the trance of linguistic close scrutiny that this book induces, terms which would simply be tiresome or embarrassing if actually employed in speech—if used by a winking wall-to-wall-carpeting salesman or an obnoxious dinner guest, say—may without warning deviate your septum here. That we manage to see them as harmless and even possibly charming is entirely to Lighter's credit; the trick seems to hinge, curiously enough, on the repeated use of a single abbreviated versicle: "usu. considered vulgar."

A *donkey dick*, for example, meaning "a frankfurter, salami, or bologna," is "usu. considered vulgar." Few observers would disagree. A *fartsack*, defined as "a sleeping bag, bedroll, bunk, cot, or bed; SACK" is, again justifiably, "usu. considered vulgar." The morning request to "Drop your cocks and grab your socks!" is "usu. considered vulgar." To *have a bug up (one's) ass [and vars.]* (meaning to "have an unreasonable, esp. obsessive or persistent, idea") is "usu. considered vulgar." A *come-pad* ("mattress") is "usu. considered vulgar." *Cunt-breath* and *dicknose* are "usu. considered vulgar." This phrase is probably the one most frequently used in the dictionary, with "usu. considered offensive" a distant second; the introductory material explains that *usu.* actually means "almost always, though not inevitably," since "'mainstream standards' are flexible and are primarily based on situation and speaker-to-speaker relationships." But the exoticizing Urdic or Swahilian symmetry of "usu." gives it comic authority, as well: it serves up each livid slangwad neatly displayed on a decorative philological doily.

What is not "usu. considered vulgar" is of some interest, too. The word *grumper* (buttocks) is not considered vulgar, perhaps because it is relatively rare. (The citation, from 1972, reads: "Some chicks lead with the boobs. . . . This chick leads with the grumper.") A *Knight of the golden grummet*, listed under *grommet* and meaning, according to a 1935 definition quoted by Lighter, "a male sexual pervert whose complex is boys," does not rate the "usu." phrase. To *deep-throat* is not vulgar. A *dingleberry* (cross-referenced with the earlier *dillberry* and *fartleberry*) painstakingly defined in a 1938 citation as "Tiny globular pieces of solidified excreta which cling to the hirsute region about the anal passage"—or, if you prefer a pithier 1966 definition, as a "piece of crap hanging on a hair"—is not flagged as vulgar, although *eagle shit* ("the gold ornamentation on the visor of a senior officer's cap") is, and *dingleberry cluster*, meaning a military decoration, does receive a "used derisively." The English, who sometimes become confused about such things, used *dingle-berries* to mean "Female breasts: low and raffish," according to Partridge, a sense that doesn't, on Lighter's evidence, seem to have reached these shores—although other unvulgar American meanings Lighter does record (and which illustrate slang's resourceful opportunism, its indifference to anatomical inconsistency) are "a doltish or contemptible person," "the testicles," "the clitoris or vagina," and "splattered molten particles around a metallic weld on a pipe or vessel."

Not only is Lighter choosy (a *chooser*, incidentally, is a neglected vaudevillism meaning "plagiarist") about what words are truly vulgar, he is also interestingly selective about what words he includes in the book at all. *Butt plug* only appears by virtue of its derisive sense, meaning a "stupid or contemptible person.—usu. considered vulgar," where it is followed by a corroborative quotation from *Beavis and Butthead*. ("Nice try, . . . butt plug.") The primary, artifactual usage of *butt plug* does not appear, apparently because it is (to quote the press release that accompanied review copies of the dictionary) "a descriptive term that cannot be said [i.e., expressed] with any other word." In Lighter's system, a word, however informal, that has no convenient synonyms probably isn't slang—*butt plug* is jargon, perhaps, a "term of art" in some advanced circles. Slang is by definition gratuitous; slang words most commonly travel in loose packs of unnecessary cognates or rhymes. (Viz., *breadhooks, cornstealers, daddles, flappers, flippers, grabbers*, and *grabhooks* for "hands"; or, for "sanatorium," *booby hatch, brain college, bughouse, cackle factory, cracker factory, fool farm, foolish factory, funny factory, funny farm, giggle academy*, and so on, all chronicled by Lighter; the bucolic "farm" variants are generally predated by the "factory" variants—idiomatic insanity in America seems to begin as an industrial symptom.) Even stand-alone units like *cookie-duster* (mustache), *crotch rocket* (motorcycle), *dusty butt* (short person), *drum snuffer* (safecracker), *blow blood* (have a nosebleed), *flannel-buzzards* (lice), or *boom bucket* (an aircraft's ejection seat) are slang by virtue of their appreciable emotional distance from, and yet complete referential synonymy with, a unit of Standard English. Only when our culture evolves at least one other word for a butt plug will the term—if I understand Lighter—merit his definitional attention.

The truth is, though, that I probably don't understand Lighter and I'm probably not doing justice to the complex algorithms that allow him to discriminate between slang and other kinds of verbal festivity. Why is *butt plug* out and *French tickler* in? If a lack of standard English synonyms is one of the tests for exclusion, why is an admittedly fine term like *gig-line* (meaning "a straight alignment of the buttons of a shirt and jacket, the belt buckle, and the fly of the trousers") included? Is there really a standard English equivalent for such a disposition of one's wardrobe? And why is *bong*, in the sense of a water-filtered pot-smoking mechanism, not to be found, while the related but more recent *bong* meaning a "device consisting of a funnel attached to a tube for drinking beer quickly" is? Lighter includes *fluff* ("the usu. passive partner in a lesbian relationship") and sister words *femme* and *fuckee*, and even *bender* ("a male homosexual who habitually assumes the passive role in anal copulation"—also known as

an *ankle grabber*), but not the related S/M sense of *bottom*.
Fender-bender, in the automotive sense, is in, as is *cluster-fuck*,
fuckhead, and even *fenderhead*, but *gender-bender* and *genderfuck*
are out—hardly surprising or scandalous omissions, although
both are interesting meldings, part of the steady slanging
down of the High Church word *gender*, which only a few
years ago was esteemed by language reformers for its lack of
connotative raciness, and which is now quietly de-euphe-
mizing, thanks to the work of genderfuck pioneers like Kate
(*neé* Albert) Bornstein, lesbian transsexual author of a play
called *Hidden: A Gender*. In the area of lit-crit and genre
studies, *fuck-book* is here (along with *dick-book* and *cunt-book*),
but *friction-fiction* is possibly too recent or too technical.

Lighter is at his most severely exclusive regarding author-
ial or journalistic neologisms. For instance, his entries for
bush, crank, and *fudge-packer* quote lines from a book of my
own, being preexistent words, whereas none of the A-
through-G novelties in that same book (*bobolinks, candy-corn,
clit-cloister, cream horns, frans*, etc.)—novelties, may I say, on
which I expensed some spirit and wasted some shame—
were allowed in. Coinages, Lighter explains, "owe their
birth partly to high spirits but chiefly to the coiner's forgiv-
able desire to impress the public with his or her wit." He
censures earlier works of reference such as Berrey and Van
den Bark's *The American Thesaurus of Slang* (1942) for including such "ephemera," contending that

> slang differs . . . from idiosyncratic wordplay and other nonce
> figuration in that it maintains a currency independent of its
> creator, the individual writer or speaker.

Lighter's experience tells him that

> Most words and phrases claimed as "slang" are nonce terms
> or "oncers," never to be seen or heard of again. Some
> become true "ghost words," recorded in slang dictionaries for
> many years but never encountered in actual usage. We have
> attempted to exclude such expressions from this dictionary.

("Ghost words" must never be confused with *ghost turds*—
"accumulations of lint found under furniture.—usu. considered vulgar.") Occasionally a fetching journalistic invention
will prosper—notably the creative work of writers at *Variety*
in the twenties and thirties, who brought us such necessi-
ties as *turkey, lay an egg,* and *flop.* But Lighter plays down the
importance of print in slang's genesis and dissemination:
"although journalism has often encouraged the spread of
slang, the chief method of popularization has always been
the shifting associational networks among individuals"—
particularly, he convincingly asserts, the associational networks within the U.S. armed services. (Lighter's command of
the history of military slang is stunning: the entry for *gook*
has over fifty citations; it is three times longer than the entry
for *chick.*) Real slang just happens: "lexical innovations are
traceable only rarely to specific persons; the proportion of
slang actually created by identifiable individuals is minute."

Despite slang's usually anonymous and often paramilitary
origins, hundreds of identifiable individuals have a place in
the *Dictionary,* doing their bit to substantiate the existence of
a given piece of loose language. Perhaps the most cheering
thing about this awesome project is how seriously it takes

the trade paperback. As one would expect, there are crumbs collected from movies, newspapers, TV series, linguistic research interviews, and celebrity profiles—as when Steve McQueen is quoted as saying, "I chickenshitted on the second turn"—but there are also innumerable illustrative quotations drawn from the work of novelists and litterateurs and even poets. Lighter and his colleagues really read books. It is a delight to encounter so many writers through their passing use of some regionalism, obscenity, or malediction. In this snickerer's *OED*, William Faulkner appears not for some high-flown word like *endure*, but for *ass-scratcher*. Sandburg is immortalized as a user of *arky malarkey*. I also ran into (in alphabetical order by term) Thomas Berger (*ass-wipe, dinkum*), Cheever (*asshole* used adjectivally), Sorrentino (*banana nose*), Eudora Welty (*bohunkus*), John Sayles (*boot* in the sense of vomit, *dead presidents*), Woody Allen (*bowels in an uproar*), Camille Paglia (*breeders*), Joseph Mitchell (*bums*), A. J. Liebling (*pain in the butt*), Philip Roth (*circle-jerker*), Harlan Ellison (*clock* and *grease-burger*), Northrop Frye (*clueless*), Barry Hannah (*cockhead, dicking off*), Henry Miller (*crap*), Kerouac (*crock-ashit*), and Erica Jong (*crotch rot*).

And there is Joseph Wambaugh (*cumbucket, don't know my dick from a dumplin*), Saul Bellow (*candy kid, cunt-struck*), Bernard Malamud (*dead-to-the-neck*), Maya Angelou (*dick-teaser*), William Burroughs (*doodle, glory hole*), Danielle Steele (*dumb cunt*), Stephen King (*el birdo, cock-knocker*), Bellow (*fart-blossom*), Hunter Thompson (*big spit*), Coover (*flagpole* meaning penis), Grace Metalious (*frig you*), John O'Hara (*frig*), S. J. Perelman (*frigged*), Edmund Wilson (*friggin'*), H. L.

Mencken (*frigging, crap*), Dos Passos (*frigging, gash*), Larry Heinemann (*fuck the duck, crapola*), Mailer (*fuck yourself, cream*), Tom Wolfe (*go-to-hell* as an adj.), Donald Barthelme (*grog*), and Robert Heinlein (*grok*, of course, but also *go cart* for "car").

Parnassian sources such as *The New York Review of Books* are not neglected either—*corn-holed* and *do* (in the sexual sense) appeared there, per Lighter. The *Atlantic Monthly* supplies the first citation for *doghouse*, musician's slang for "double-bass" (1920). *Esquire* pops up as a locus for a rare 1976 use of *dog water*, which, Lighter informs us, means "clear drops of seminal fluid." *The New Yorker* makes many appearances, some for nice old words like *brads* ("cash"), *cluckhead*, and *cheesy*. (Lighter's crew has, by the way, come up with a sentence employing *cheesy* that predates by over thirty years the first *cheesy* citation in the Supplement to the *OED*. In 1863 someone named Massett wrote: "The orchestra consisting of the fiddle—a very cheezy flageolet, played by a gentlemen with one eye—a big drum, and a triangle.") *The New Yorker* also substantiates the word *fucking* used adverbially, thanks to its recent explosion of profanity, and it furnishes two separate nuances of *asshole* dating from 1993.

For obvious reasons, though, the magazine that is most often quoted in *The Historical Dictionary of American Slang* is *The National Lampoon*. Lighter and his crew have combed its back issues carefully in quest of elusive flannel-buzzards, and they have not gone unrewarded. Yet here the editors must have had difficulty at times deciding which words were merely "nonce figuration," to be excluded from the dictionary, and which words had obtained a "currency independent of the speaker." The fact that *The National Lampoon* uses *cock-locker* or *flog the dolphin* or *get your bananas peeled* (all with sexual meanings) is taken to be an indication that this recherché vocabulary enjoyed a currency independent of the humorist during the period in question. It may have; *Lampoon* writers were expert listeners and diligent field-workers. But they were, as well, habitués of the reference room; in some cases at least, one suspects that they simply pulled down a few slang tomes, found a "ghost word" they thought was funny, and resurrected it for the greater good. P. J. O'Rourke recently told a lunch-table that he owns a whole shelf of unconventional lexicography; he and Michael O'Donohue, another *Lampoon* contributor and professional slangfarber, were particularly fond of one major thesaurus dating from (he thought) the thirties—by which he surely meant Berrey and Van den Bark's huge "ephemera"-filled collection from the forties. In this way, out of the dried mud-flats of old reference books, to one-time creative placement in a humor magazine, to further climate-controlled stasis in Lighter's *Dictionary*, are some words blessed with "currency" after a single recycling. And the language is happier for it.

Using *The Historical Dictionary of American Slang* will prob-ably have long-term side effects. A three-week self-immersion in Lighter's initial volume significantly altered this suggestible reader's curse-patterns. I swore more often and more incom-prehensibly while reading it than ever before; the "Captain Haddock syndrome" was especially noticeable while driv-ing. (Captain Haddock is the character in the Tintin series who, when drunk, showers puzzling nonce-abuse on people:

Poltroons! Iconoclasts! Bashi-bazouks!) To a slow motorist (with windows closed, of course, so he couldn't hear), I would call out, "*Go*, you little scum-jockey!"—or "corn-pad" or "dirt-bonnet." None of these formulae is to be found in Lighter (at least, there is no reason to expect *scum-jockey* to appear in Volume III), but reading Volume I made me say them. Furthermore, under Lighter's fluid spell I spent several hours working on a matrix of related insults:

You		bag!	ball!	bomb!	wad!	wipe!	loaf!
	cheese-		x		?	?	?
	corn-		x		?	?	
	dirt-	x	x	x			
	grease-		x				
	hose-	x			x	?	
	jiz-	x			x	x	?
	scum-	x	x		x		
	scuzz-	x	x			x	?
	sleaze-	x	x	x	x		
	slime-		x		x		

(An *x* indicates an existing piece of slang; a question mark indicates a plausible compound, which may or may not appear in the future. Whether there is any linguistic point to building such a predictive matrix is an open question.)

Some of these behavioral aberrations will pass in time, but it is at least possible that by the spring of 1997, when the final installment of this mighty triptych assumes its place in the library, those of us who have been diligently reading and waiting will discover ourselves to be marginally better people, or at least more cheerful and enlightened and tolerant swearers, as a result of what Jonathan Lighter and his cohorts have done for the massive and heretofore unmanageable dirtball of American slang.

(1994)

READING ALOUD

A few years ago I did my first reading. It was at the Edinburgh Festival in Scotland, under a tent. Several others read, too; we all sat on independent sections of a biomorphic orange modular couch, our heads bowed as we listened, or half listened, to each other. Eventually my turn came, and the words that I had written in silence (an earplug-enhanced silence, as a matter of fact, that amplified the fleeting Chiclety contact of upper and lower incisors, and made audible the inner squirt of an eyeball when I rubbed it roughly, and called to my attention the muffled roar of eyelid muscles when my eyes were squeezed shut in an effort to see, using the infrared of prose, whatever it was that I most wanted at that moment to describe)—these formerly silent words unfolded themselves like lawn chairs in my mouth and emerged one by one wearing large Siberian hats of consonants and long erminous vowels and landed softly, without visible damage, here and there in the audience, and I thought, Gosh, I'm reading aloud, from Chapter Seven!

Things went pretty well until I got to a place near the middle of the last paragraph, where I began to feel that I was

going to cry. I wouldn't have minded crying, or at least pausing to swallow down a discreet silent sob, if what I'd been
reading had been in any obvious way sad. When people on
TV documentaries tell their stories, and they come to the
part where the tragedy happens and they have to say over
again what, in silent form, they adjusted to years earlier, and
they choke up, that's fine, they should choke up. And I've
heard writers read autobiographical accounts of painful
childhood events and quaver a little here and there—that's
perfectly justifiable, even desirable. But the sentence that was
giving me difficulty was a description of a woman enclosing
a breakfast muffin in bakery tissue, placing it in a small bag,
and sprinkling it with coffee stirrers and sugar packets and
pre-portioned pats of butter. Where was the pathos? And
yet by the time I delivered the words "plastic stirrers" to the
audience, I was in serious trouble, and I noticed a listening
head or two look up with sudden curiosity: Hah, this is interesting, this American is going to weep openly and copiously
for us now.

Why that sentence, though? Why did that image of a succession of small white shapes, more stirrers and sugar packets and butter pats than I needed, and in that sense ceremonial
and semi-decorative rather than functional, falling, falling
over my terrestrial breakfast, grab at my grief-lapels? There
were a number of reasons. In college I had once competed
for a prize in what was called the "Articulation of the English Language," for which the contestants had to read aloud
from set passages of Milton and Joyce and others. I got to
the auditorium late, having bicycled there while drinking
proudly from a shot bottle of Smirnoff vodka that I'd bought

on an airplane, and, as planned, I read the Milton in a boom-
ing fake English accent and read the Joyce excerpt—which
was the last paragraph of "The Dead"—first in a broad bad
Southern accent, then in a Puerto Rican accent, and then in
the Southern accent again, and to my surprise I'd found that
the Joyce suddenly seemed, in my amateur TV-actor drawl,
extremely moving, so that the last phrase, about the snow
"faintly falling . . . upon all the living and the dead," was
tragic enough to make it unclear whether my rhetorical
tremor was genuine or not—and my voice box may have
remembered this boozy Joycean precipitation from college
as I read aloud from my own sugar-packet snowfall.

Also, a version of the chapter I was reading in Edinburgh
had appeared in *The New Yorker,* and I'd had a slight disagreement, a friendly disagreement, with a fact checker there
over the phrase "tissue-protected muffin." She'd held that
the word "tissue" implied something like Kleenex, and that
it should be a "paper-wrapped muffin," and I'd said I didn't
think so. On the way home from work the next day I'd
stopped in a bakery and spotted a blue box of the little squares
in question and I'd seen the words "bakery tissue" in capital
letters on the side; and, exulting, I'd called the manager of
the store over, a Greek man who barely spoke English, and
offered to buy the entire box, which he sold me for nine
dollars, and I called my editor the next day and said, "It's tissue, it is tissue," and as a compromise it became in their version a "tissue-wrapped muffin"—but now, reading it aloud
in Scotland, I could turn it into a "tissue-protected muffin"
all over again; right or wrong, I was able in the end to shield
the original wordless memory from alien breakfast guests with

this fragile shroud of my own preferred words. It had turned out all right in the end. And that might have been enough to make me cry.

But it wasn't just that. It was also that this tiny piece of a paragraph had never been one that I'd thought of proudly when I thought over my book after it was published. I'd forgotten it, after writing it down, and now that my orating tongue forced me to pay attention to it I was amazed and moved that it had hung in there for all those months, in fact years, unrewarded but unimpaired, holding its small visual charge without any further encouragement from me, and, like the deaf and dumb kid in rags who, though reviled by the other children, ends up saving his village from some catastrophe, it had become the tearjerker moment that would force me, out of pity for its very unmemorableness, to dissolve in grief right in the midst of all my intended ironies. That was a big part of it.

Contrition, too. Contrition made its contribution to the brimming bowl—for these Edinburgh audience members didn't know how much pure mean-spirited contempt I had felt back in my rejection-letter days for writers who "gave readings," how self-congratulatorily neo-primitivist I'd thought it was to repudiate the divine economy of the published page and to require people to gather to hear a reticent man or woman reiterate what had long since been set in type. Ideally, I'd felt, the republic of letters was inhabited by solitary readers in bed with their Itty Bitty Book Lights glowing over their privately owned and operated pages, like the ornate personal lamps that covertly illuminate every music stand in opera pits while the crudest sort of public melodrama rages in heavy makeup overhead. There was something a bit too Pre-Raphaelite about the regression to an audience—I thought of those reaction shots in early Spielberg movies, of family members gazing with softly awestruck faces at the pale-green glow of the beneficent UFO while John Williams flogged yet more Strauss from his string section. And there were the suspect intonation patterns, the I'm-reading-aloud patterns—especially at poetry readings, where talented and untalented alike, understandably wishing in the absence of rhyme to give an audible analogue for the ragged right and left margins in their typed or printed original, resorted to syllable-punching rhythms and studiously unresolved final cadences adapted from Dylan Thomas and Wallace Stevens, overlaid with Walter Cronkite and John Fitzgerald Kennedy. These handy tonal templates could make anything lyrical:

> This—is a Dover—edition—
> Designed—for years—of use—
>
> Sturdy stackable—beechwood—bookshelves—
> At a price you'd expect—to pay—for plastic—

And yet, despite all this sort of easy, Glenn-Gouldy contempt in my background, there I was physically in Edinburgh, under that tent, among strangers, finishing up my own first reading, and, far from feeling dismissive and contemptuous before my turn came, I'd been simply and sincerely nervous, exceedingly nervous, and now I was almost finished, and I hadn't done anything too humiliating, and the audience had innocently listened, unaware of my prior disapproval, and they had even tolerantly laughed once or twice—and all this was too much: I was like a crippled unbeliever wheeled in and made whole with a sudden palm blow to the forehead by a preaching charlatan. I'm reading aloud! I'm reading aloud! I was saying, my face streaming with tears—I was cripple and charlatan simultaneously. Evidently I was going to cry, out of pure gratitude to myself for having gotten almost to the end without crying.

And then, as the unthinkable almost happened, and the narcissus bulb in the throat very nearly blossomed, I recognized that if I did break down now, the intensity of my feeling, in this supposedly comic context, would leave the charitable listeners puzzled about my overall mental well-being. At the very least I would be thought of as someone "going through a stressful time," and it would be this diagnosis they would take home with them, rather than any particular fragment from what I'd read that they liked, and whenever I tried to write something light 'n' lively thereafter I would remember my moment of shame on the orange couch and to counteract it I'd have to invent something bleak and brooding and wholly out of character. I couldn't let it happen; I couldn't let reading aloud distort my future output. I started whispering urgent ringside counsel to myself: *Come on, you sack of shit. If you cry, people will assume you're being moved to tears by your own eloquence, and how do you think that will go over?* That was frightening enough, finally, to stabilize the nutation in my Adam's apple, and I just barely got through to the last word.

Since that afternoon in 1989, I've read aloud from my

writing a number of times, and each time I've been a little
more in control, less of a walking cripple, more of a charlatan. I've reacquainted myself with my larynx. When I was
fourteen I used to feel it each morning at the kitchen table,
before I had any cereal. It was large. How could my throat
have been retrofitted with this massive service elevator? And
what was I going to say with it? What sort of payloads was
it fated to carry? First thing in the morning I could sing, in
a fairly convincing baritone, the alto-sax solo from *Pictures at
an Exhibition*—and as I went for a low note there was a
unique physical pleasure, not to be had later in the day,
when the two thick slack vocal cords dropped and closed on
a shovelful of sonic peat moss. Sometimes as I sang low, or
swung low, it felt as if I were a character actor in a coffee
commercial, carelessly scooping glossy beans from deep in a
burlap bag and pouring them into a battered scale—the
deeper the note I tried to scoop up, the bigger and glossier
the beans, until finally I was way down in fava territory. I
was Charles Kuralt, I was Tony the Tiger, I was Lloyd
Bridges, I was James Earl Jones—I too had a larynx the size
of a picnic basket, I felt, and when you heard my voice you
wouldn't even know it was sound, it would be so vibrantly
low: you'd think instead that your wheels had strayed over
the wake-up rumble strips on the shoulder of a freeway. Just
above the mobile prow of the Adam's apple, just above
where there should properly be a hood ornament, was a
softer place that became more noticeable to the finger the
lower you spoke or sang, and it was directly into this vul-
nerable opening, this chink in the armor of one's virility,
that I imagined disc jockeys secretly injecting themselves

with syringes full of male hormones and small-engine oil, so that they could say "traffic and weather together" with the proper sort of sawtooth bite.

And though my own voice has proved to be—despite my high secondary-sexual expectations, and even though I was pretty tall and tall people often have voice boxes to match— not quite the pebbly, three-dimensional mood machine I'd counted on, I do occasionally now like reading aloud what I've written. I get back a little of the adolescent early-morning feeling as I brachiate my way high into the upper canopy of a sentence, tightening the pitch muscles, climbing up, and then dropping on a single word, with that Doppler-effect plunge of sound, so the argument can live out its closing seconds at sea level. I feel all this going on, even if it isn't audi- ble to anyone else. And sometimes I know that my voice, imperfect medium though it may be, is making what I've written seem for the moment better than it is, and I like playing with this dangerous intonational power, and even letting listeners know that I'm playing with it. It's not called an Adam's apple for nothing: that relic of temptation, that articulated chunk of upward mobility, that ever-ready dial tone in the throat, whether or not it successfully leads oth- ers astray, ends by thoroughly seducing oneself.

(1992)

LUMBER

Now feels like a good time to pick a word or a phrase, something short, and go after it, using the available equipment of intellectual retrieval, to see where we get. A metaphor might work best—one that has suggested itself over a few centuries with just the right frequency: not so often that its recovered uses prove to be overwhelming or trivial, nor so seldom that it hasn't had a chance to refine and extend its meaning in all kinds of indigenous foliage. It should be representatively out of the way; it should have seen better days. Once or twice in the past it briefly enjoyed the status of a minor cliché, but now, for one reason or another, it is ignored or forgotten. Despite what seems to be a commonplace exterior, the term ought to be capable of some fairly deep and marimbal timbres when knowledgeably struck. A distinct visual image should accompany it, and yet ideally its basic sense should be easily misunderstood, since the merging of such elementary misconstruals will help contribute to its accumulated drift. It should lead us beyond itself, and back to itself. And it should sometimes be beautiful.

The mind has been called a *lumber-room*, and its contents or its printed products described as *lumber*, since about 1680. Mind-lumber had its golden age in the eighteenth century, became hackneyed by the late nineteenth century, and went away by 1970 or so. I know this because I've spent almost a year, on and off, riffling in the places that scholars and would-be scholars go when they want to riffle: in dictionaries, indexes, bibliographies, biographies, concordances, catalogs, anthologies, encyclopedias, dissertation abstracts, library stacks, full-text CD-ROMs, electronic bulletin boards, and online electronic books; also in books of quotations, collections of aphorisms, old thesauruses, used-book stores, and rare-book rooms; and (never to be slighted, even if, in my own case, a habitual secretiveness limits their usefulness) in other living minds, too—since "Learned men" (so William D'Avenant wrote in 1650, when the art of indexing was already well advanced) "have been to me the best and briefest Indexes of Books"; or, as John Donne sermonized in 1626, "The world is a great Volume, and man the Index of that Booke."

Boswell, for example, said, in the last pages of his biography, that Johnson's superiority over other learned men "consisted chiefly in what may be called the art of thinking,"

the art of using his mind; a certain continual power of seizing the useful substance of all that he knew, and exhibiting it in a clear and forcible manner; so that knowledge, which we often see to be no better than lumber in men of dull understanding, was, in him, true, evident, and actual wisdom.

Logan Pearsall Smith, in an essay on the sermons of John Donne, asserts that the seventeenth-century divines, "with all the lumber they inherited from the past, inherited much also that gives an enduring splendour to their works." Michael Sadleir, in his *The Northanger Novels: A Footnote to Jane Austen* (1927), writes: "There are probably no items in the lumber-rooms of forgotten literature more difficult to trace than the minor novels of the late eighteenth century." One of those minor novels was Charles Johnstone's *Chrysal* (1760–65), in which a bookseller named Mr. Vellum stores surplus copies of books by a dead self-published author for seven years in the "lumber garret" so that he can pass them off as new creations. Laurence Sterne mentions "the lumber-rooms of learning" in Book IV of *Tristram Shandy* (1761).

Goethe revered Sterne, and he might have read *Chrysal* (which was translated into German in 1775); and Goethe's learned yearner, Faust, calls the spirit of the past, as it is reflected in the minds who study it, a *Kehrichtfaß* and a *Rumpelkammer*, in a line that has been variously Englished as a "mouldy dustbin, or a lumber attic" (Philip Wayne), "a junk heap,/A lumber room" (Randall Jarrell), "Mere scraps of odds and ends, old crazy lumber,/In dust-bins only fit to rot and slumber" (Theodore Martin, revised by W. H. Bruford), "A very lumber-room, a rubbish-hole" (Anna Swanwick), "A heap of rubbish, and a lumber room" (John Stuart Blackie), "A rubbish-bin, a lumber-garret" (George Madison Priest), "A trash bin and a lumber-garret" (Stuart Atkins), "An

offal-barrel and a lumber-garret" (Bayard Taylor), "a trash
barrel and a junk room" (Bayard Quincy Morgan), "A lumber-
room and a rubbish heap" (Louis MacNeice and E. L. Stahl),
and "A mass of things confusedly heaped together;/A lumber-room of dusty documents" (John Anster). Lord Francis
Leveson Gower's early translation (John Murray, 1823) may
be, for this particular passage, the best:

> Read but a paragraph, and you shall find
> The litter and the lumber of the mind.[1]

Master Humphrey has lumber dreams in the first chapter
of Dickens's *Old Curiosity Shop*:

But all that night, waking or in my sleep, the same thoughts
recurred and the same images retained possession of my
brain. I had ever before me the old dark murky rooms—the
gaunt suits of mail with their ghostly silent air—the faces all
awry, grinning from wood and stone—the dust and rust, the
worm that lives in wood—and alone in the midst of all this

---

[1]Gower's translation offers a bonus *lumber* earlier that is almost as inspiring:

> Hemm'd round with learning's musty scrolls,
> Her ponderous volumes, dusty rolls,
> Which to the ceiling's vault arise,
> Above the reach of studious eyes,
> Where revelling worms peruse the store
> Of wisdom's antiquated lore,—
> With glasses, tools of alchemy,
>   Cases and bottles, whole and crack'd,
>   Hereditary lumber, pack'd.
> This is the world, the world, for me!

lumber and decay, and ugly age, the beautiful child in her
gentle slumber, smiling through her light and sunny dreams.

Hazlitt does not refer to the lumber of scholarship where
you would expect him to, in his Montaignesque "On the
Ignorance of the Learned," but he does so, affectionately, in
"On Pedantry," an essay that also contains his helpful circular definition of learning as "the knowledge of that which is
not generally known." Of a character named Keith in *South
Wind*, Norman Douglas writes, "He had an encyclopaedic
turn of mind; his head, as somebody once remarked, was a
lumber-room of useless information."

Norman Douglas's "somebody" was probably Lord
Chesterfield, who in 1748 advised his son that "Many great
readers load their memories without exercising their judg-
ments, and make lumber-rooms of their heads, instead of
furnishing them usefully." Sir Thomas Browne, though he
was one of the greatest of readers, and of indexers, claimed
to have avoided this pitfall: "I make not therefore my head a
grave, but a treasure, of knowledge," he writes, in *Religio
Medici* (1642), finding no use here for the word "lumber,"[1]
but getting some mileage instead out of the Greek root of
thesaurus—"treasure-house"—a word associated with dictionaries long before Roget,[2] and employed in passing in an
eighteenth-century Latin oration written by Johann Mencken
(and edited by a collateral descendant, H. L. Mencken) called
The Charlatanry of the Learned:

[1]Not every passage quoted herein will actually contain the word; that would
be obsessive.

[2]Cf. Thomas Cooper's *Thesaurus Linguae Romanae & Britannicae, 1565*.

The bookshops are full of Thesauruses of Latin Antiquities which, when examined, turned out to be far less treasuries than fuel for the fire.

Mencken himself, in his autobiographical "Larval Stage of a Bookworm," said that

At eight or nine, I suppose, intelligence is no more than a small spot of light on the floor of a large and murky room.

This is Mencken's elegantly spare version of John Locke's *dark room*, from *An Essay Concerning Human Understanding* (1690), which is illuminated by shafts of external and internal sensation:

These alone, as far as I can discover, are the windows by which light is let into this *dark room*. For, methinks, the understanding is not much unlike a closet wholly shut from light, with only some little opening left, to let in external visible resemblances, or ideas of things without. . . . [Locke's italics.]

And Locke's unlit closet may be an irreligious revision of the room of despair, "a very dark room, where there sat a man in an iron cage," in Bunyan's *Pilgrim's Progress* (1678).[1]

___

[1]Both Locke's and Bunyan's *dark rooms* may owe something to a sermon by John Donne delivered on Christmas Day, 1624: "God does not furnish a roome, and leave it darke; he sets up lights in it; his first care was, that his benefits should be seene; he made light first, and then creatures, to be seene by that light. . . ."

Practicing architects had tired, by the 1890s, of dark seventeenth-century rooms of the soul, and had developed as a result an antipathy to the closet. Russell Sturgis, in an article on "The Equipment of the Modern City House," appearing in *Harper's Magazine* in April 1899, mentions one architect who wanted to rid domestic life of closets altogether, arguing that they were

> extremely wasteful of space, and in every way to be shunned; that they were places where old lumber was stored and forgotten, dust-catchers, nests for vermin, fire-traps.

But one has to store things somewhere; and Sherlock Holmes in 1887 compared the brain in its untutored state to a "little empty attic," which should be properly stocked:

> A fool takes in all the lumber of every sort that he comes across, so that the knowledge which might be useful to him gets crowded out, or at best is jumbled up with a lot of other things, so that he has a difficulty in laying his hands upon it. *(A Study in Scarlet.)*

Holmes warns Watson that "it is a mistake to think that that little room has elastic walls and can distend to any extent." Montaigne, however, disagrees: when considering the question whether (in Florio's translation, "Of Pedantisme") "a mans owne wit, force, droope, and as it were diminish it selfe, to make roome for others," he at first appears to hold that it does, and then he decides that, no, on the contrary, "our mind stretcheth the more by how much more it is replenished."

———————

These preliminary examples and semirelevant corollaries, having stretched the elastic walls of the preceding paragraphs nearly to the point of tissue damage, must now draw back to reveal, in a kind of establishing quotational shot, the one really famous piece of lumber we have. It was published in 1711, the work of the twenty-three-year-old Alexander Pope. (Youth is often a time of lumber: "An ever increasing volume of dimensional lumber is juvenile wood," as Timothy D. Larson pointed out in 1992, in his "The Mechano-Sorptive Response of Juvenile Wood to Hygrothermal Gradients," indexed in the *Dissertation Abstracts* CD-ROM.[1]) Pope's *An Essay on Criticism* describes a bad critic:

> The Bookful Blockhead, ignorantly read
> With Loads of Learned Lumber in his Head.

This is a very good couplet: *ignorantly* fills its allotted verse-hole with a lumpy tumultuousness, like a rudely twisted paper clip, and the three capital Ls on the next line halt in their places one after another as remuneratively as a triplet of twirling Lemons in a slot machine just before the quarters start spraying out. Pope's jingle has stayed with us: it is included under the heading "Reading: Its Dangers" in *The*

———

[1] Juvenile wood is wood near the pith of the tree; it has a "larger longitudinal hygrocoefficient of expansion than mature wood," writes Larson, who is concerned that the expansion-habits of juvenile wood will lead to "an increase in the frequency and severity in spatial deformation of wood subjected to hygrothermal gradients."

Home Book of Quotations; it appears in *Bartlett's* and *The Oxford Dictionary of Quotations*. Even in extrapoetical contexts it continues to find advocates: as recently as 1989 (so the *Wilson Library Literature* CD-ROM index points out), Peter A. Hoare contributed a chapter to *The Modern Academic Library: Essays in Memory of Philip Larkin* that was called "Loads of Learned Lumber: Special Collections in the Smaller University Library." Hoare writes that specialized collections, regardless of whether they are directly related to any "immediate academic programme," nonetheless "contribute, not always in an easily definable way, to the quality of the whole institution"; and he mentions Larkin's useful distinction between the "magical value" and the "meaningful value" of literary manuscripts.

Where in *his* library, though, one wants to ask, did Pope find his *lumber*? Pope was an artful borrower, a mechanosorptive wonder, as generations of often testy commentators have shown; many of his finest metrical sub-units have an isolable source. (E.g., Pope's "Windsor Forest" mentions a "sullen Mole, that hides his diving Flood," which rodent is, says commentator Wakefield, a borrowing, or burrowing, from Milton's "Vacation Exercise," where there is a "sullen Mole that runneth underneath.") Is *learned lumber* from Milton, too, then?

No, it isn't. Milton didn't use *lumber* in any poem, and you will find it (with the aid of Sterne and Kollmeier's *Concordance to the English Prose of John Milton*, 1985) only once in all his prose works: "When Ministers came to have Lands, Houses, Farmes, Coaches, Horses, and the like Lumber," he says in *Eikonklastes* (1649), "then Religion brought forth riches in the Church, and the Daughter devour'd the Mother." Is Pope's *lumber* from Shakespeare, then, or Spenser, or Marlowe, or Urquhart's translation of Rabelais? Can it really be that he coined the phrase himself? The critical editions of Pope—even the great Twickenham series that came out piecemeal while Nabokov was working on *Pale Fire* (1962) and his Pushkin commentary—suggest no specific sources in this case; E. Audra and Aubrey Williams, the Twickenham editors of *An Essay on Criticism*, confine themselves to a footnote citing the *Oxford English Dictionary: "Lumber* 'useless or cumbrous material' (OED)." Is it from Horace or Quintilian, in the original or in translation? (Lady Mary Wortley Montagu: "I admired Mr. Pope's Essay on Criticism at first, very much, because I had not then read any of the ancient critics, and did not know that it was all stolen.") Is it from Jonathan Swift?

Swift does indeed have a passage in his early "Ode to Sir William Temple" that goes

> Let us (for shame) no more be fed
> With antique Reliques of the Dead,
> The Gleanings of Philosophy,
> Philosophy! the Lumber of the Schools
> The Roguery of Alchymy,
>   And we the bubbled Fools
> Spend all our present Stock in hopes of golden Rules.

This was written around 1692—the *Oxford Dictionary of Quotations* quotes just its fourth line—but the ode remained unprinted until 1745, when it was included in one of Dodsley's *Miscellanies*; it isn't likely that Pope read it until after he had published *An Essay on Criticism* (1711, 1711—I must try to remember that date) and had befriended Swift. Swift's first published poem, his "Ode to the Athenian Society" (1692), is a potential influence; it praises the efforts on the part of the Athenian Society[1] to strip Philosophy, that "beauteous Queen," of her old lumber:

> Her Face patch'd o'er with Modern Pedantry,
>> With a long sweeping Train
> Of Comments and Disputes, ridiculous and vain,
>> All of old Cut with a new Dye,
>> How soon have You restor'd her Charms!
> And rid her of her Lumber and Her Books,
>> Drest her again Genteel and Neat,
>>> And rather Tite than Great,
> How fond we are to court Her to our Arms!
> How much of Heav'n is in her naked looks.

Despite the naked looks, this setting of *lumber* (which I found using the *Concordance to the Poems of Jonathan Swift*, edited by Michael Shinagel, 1972) is also comparatively humdrum—

---

[1] Samuel Johnson, in his "Life of Swift," described the Athenian Society as "a knot of obscure men." They were Samuel Wesley (whom we will meet again later), Daniel Defoe, and the publisher John Dunton, among others; they published Swift's flattering "Ode" in their *Athenian Gazette*, vol. 5, supplement, 1692. Dunton wrote that Swift's "Ode" was "an ingenious poem" (See John Nichols, *Literary Anecdotes of the Eighteenth Century*, ed. Colin Clair, p. 122), but Pat Rogers (*Jonathan Swift: The Complete Poems*, p. 604) reports that Joseph Horrell's harsh verdict—that this is Swift's "worst poem by odds"—is "shared by many critics."

not capable on its own of inspiring Pope's magnificently
punched-up lumber-couplet. And Swift's early prose is no
help, either. In *Tale of a Tub* (1704) there is the interesting
brain-recipe for distilling calfbound books in an alchemical
solution of *balneo Mariae*, poppy, and Lethe and then "snuffing it strongly up your nose" while setting to work on your
critical treatise, whereupon (in another variation on the
notion of the brain as a treasure-house and thesaurus)

> you immediately perceive in your head an infinite number
> of *abstracts, summaries, compendiums, extracts, collections, medu-
> las, excerpta quaedams, florilegias* and the like, all disposed into
> great order, and reducible upon paper.

Amid these rudenesses about modern erudition, however,
not one lumbered disparagement, perplexingly, appears.
We can be sure of the absence, since there is nothing
listed between *ludicrously* and *lungs* in Kelling and Preston's
computer-generated *KWIC Concordance to Jonathan Swift's A
Tale of a Tub, The Battle of the Books, and A Discourse Concerning the Mechanical Operation of the Spirit* (1984). (KWIC stands
for Key Word In Context.) It could be that Swift felt less
inclined to use the word "lumber" after he showed Dryden
his Athenian "Ode" and Dryden said to him (as Johnson
tells it), "Cousin Swift, you will never be a poet." Dryden,
after all, had himself been a lumberer of some prominence
in his day: "We bring you none of our old lumber hither,"
the Poet Laureate promised the King and Queen, on behalf
of a newly consolidated dramatic company, in 1682; and in
his prologue to *Mr. Limberham* (1680) he complains that

True wit has seen its best days long ago;
It ne'er looked up, since we were dipt in show;
When sense in doggrel rhymes and clouds was lost,
And dulness flourished at the actor's cost.
Nor stopt it here; when tragedy was done,
Satire and humour the same fate have run,
And comedy is sunk to trick and pun.
Now our machining lumber will not sell,
And you no longer care for heaven or hell;
What stuff will please you next, the Lord can tell.

("Machining lumber" means clunky theatrical supernatural-ism and personification, *deus ex machinery*.) To Swift the word would have felt like a piece of Dryden's proprietary vocabulary, and, wounded by Dryden's brutal assessment of his literary future, he purged it from his speech for over twenty years.[1] Or maybe not.

Either way, Swift and Dryden don't look to be convincing sources for Pope's durable phrase. Is it from Samuel Butler's *Hudibras*, which Swift had by heart, or did Pope get it from Francis Bacon's *New Atlantis*, or from a sermon by Donne or Jeremy Taylor, or from John Locke? ("Locke's reasoning may indeed be said to pervade every part of the *Essay on Criticism*," writes Courthope, another nineteenth-century Pope commentator.) And, more elementarily—before we get too

---

[1] There is no *lumber* in *Gulliver's Travels* (1726). The word resurfaces in Swift's "The Progress of Poetry," written c. 1719 but not published until the *Miscellanies in Prose and Verse* (1728), which was edited by Pope: "To raise the lumber from the earth." Pat Rogers subjoins a note to this line: "*lumber* one of Pope's favourite terms of opprobrium."

carried away in our snuffing for sources—what exactly does
the word "lumber" *mean* in Pope's poetry, and in poetry generally? Do we really understand what Pope has in mind,
metaphorically, when he refers to "Loads of Learned Lumber"? What might these loads look like? Edwin Abbott's
Concordance to the Works of Alexander Pope (1875) helpfully
gives, in addition to the "learned" line, three later settings for
"lumber," all from *The Dunciad,* two of which employ the
word nominatively, in the relevant anti-pedantic sense:

Lumber.

Dropt the dull *l.* of the Latin store *D.* iv. 319
With loads of learned *l.* in his head *E.C.* 613
Thy giddy Dulness still shall l. *on D.* iii. 294
A l.-house *of books in ev'ry head D.* iii. 193

Edwin A. Abbott writes, in his introduction to the concordance his father compiled, "I venture to commend the following pages to all those who wish to be able to know at any
moment how Pope used any English word in his Original
Poems." And who would not want to know at any moment
how Pope, of all poets—one of the most skilled word-pickers
and word-packers in literary history—used any English word?
Who does not feel an inarticulate burble of gratitude toward
the senior Mr. Abbott (1808–1882; headmaster of the Philological School, Marylebone) for the enormous manual labor
he expended in copying and sorting Pope's lines, creating a
book that, though few will read it cover to cover, selflessly
paves the sophomore's strait path to pedantry? Concordances
are true triumphs of what Michael Gruber, a pseudonymous

thriller writer and marine biologist, recently called "sift-ware"[1]—they are quote verifiers and search engines that in an ardent inquirer's hands sometimes turn up poetical secrets that the closest of close readings would not likely uncover.[2]

But grateful though we must always be to Edwin Abbott, the truth is that in the case of *lumber*, at least, his grand Victorian concordance fails us—fails us because it indexes only from the revised, final version of *The Dunciad* (1743). It does not include a more revealing use of *lumber* that appears in the first, and at times superior, *Dunciad* of 1728.

The searcher *will* find this particular couplet, though, in the beautiful, blue *Concordance to the Poems of Alexander Pope*, in two volumes, by Emmett Bedford and Robert Dilligan, produced in 1974 with the help of a Univac 1108 and an

[1]See the WELL's "Info" Conference ("A Conference About Communication Systems, Communities, and Tools for the Information Age"), Topic 641 ("Internet Encyclopedia"), Response 15 (Oct. 26, 1993): "Your hyperencyclopedia software (or 'siftware') would direct you toward a basic article on spiders, analogous to the FAQ files placed in many newsgroups." The WELL is an electronic conferencing system: (415) 332-8410; http://www.well.com.

[2]Inspired by Kent Hieatt's numerical analysis of Edmund Spenser's "Epithalamion" (*Short Time's Endless Monument*, 1960), a sophomore in college, in 1975, wrote a paper on the numerical structure of Book I of *The Faery Queen*, in which he pointed out that the word *seven* appears for the first time in the poem on line seven, stanza 17, Canto vii of Spenser's poem ("For seven great heads out of his body grew"), and appears in precisely the same context (a mention of the seven-headed beast that carries the Whore of Babylon) as surrounds the word *seven* in Revelations chapter 17, verse 7. Without Osgood's concordance to Spenser (1915) and several concordances to the Bible open before him, the student would never have noticed this further tiny instance of Spenserian numerology. And it was so incredibly *easy*, too, once I (for it was I) had decided what to look up: "Index-learning," Pope himself pointed out, reworking some earlier snideries of Charles Boyle and Dean Swift,

> turns no student pale,
> Yet holds the Eel of science by the Tail.

IBM 370 computer, using optically scanned microfilm images of the Twickenham edition.[1] Alternatively, you can find the couplet that Abbott omitted as I first found it, by peering into the greatest lumber-room, or lumber-ROM, ever constructed: the all-powerful, manually keyed *English Poetry Full-Text Database*, released in June of 1994 on four silver disks the size of Skilsaw blades by the prodigious Eel of Science himself, Sir Charles Chadwyck-Healey.

Chadwyck-Healey's forces are responsible for a variety of CD-ROM power-tools: they have brought us the National Security Archive Index of previously classified documents; the catalog of the British Library to 1975; full texts of *The Economist, The Times, The Guardian, Il Sole 24 Ore*, and works of African-American literature; indexes of periodicals, films, music, and French theses; the full text of the nine-volume *Grand Robert de la Langue Française*; United Nations records indexed or in full text, auction records, Hansard's record of the House of Commons, a world climate disk, and British census data; all 221 volumes of Migne's *Patrologia Latina*; on and on. But nothing can remotely compare, in range and depth and tantric power, with their *English Poetry Database*, which promises, and moreover delivers, something like 4,500

---

[1] Soberingly, the editors of the concordance write that "this optical scanning proved to be the phase of the project that caused the most problems and it seemed for a time that we had traded a tedious but straightforward task [i.e., manual text-entry] for an exasperatingly complicated one. . . . But these difficulties were related to the fact that the technique of direct optical scanning, the claims of computer and data processing houses to the contrary, is still in the developmental stage. Our experience with this method makes us feel that for most purposes literary scholars had best regard it as in the realm of the possible as contrasted with the practical."

volumes of liquidly, intimately friskable poetry by 1,350 poets who wrote between A.D. 600 and 1900.

Not that it is all English poetry: "all" is a meaningless word to use in connection with so sprawling a domain. "Nowhere in our publicity do we say that we are including every poem ever written or published in the English language," writes Alison Moss, Chadwyck-Healey's editorial director, in a newsletter; and the project consciously sidestepped certain squishy areas: American poetry, drama, verse annuals and miscellanies (with some important exceptions), and poems by writers not listed or cross-referenced as poets in the *New Cambridge Bibliography of English Literature*. The project's heavy reliance on this last-mentioned work has led to some puzzling exclusions. While the *English Poetry Database* includes a truly astounding and thrilling number of minor poems by minor poets, it is unreliable in its coverage of minor poems, and in some cases major poems, by major prose writers.

"I shall not insult you by insinuating that you do not remember Scott's *Lay of the Last Minstrel*," wrote Vladimir Nabokov in the top margin of page 37 of his teaching copy of *Madame Bovary*[1]; but Walter Scott's poem is not to be found in the *English Poetry Database*.[2] The poem by the nineteenth-century *Erewhon*-man, Samuel Butler, about a plaster cast of a Greek discus-thrower kept prudishly in storage,

[1]Reproduced in *Lectures on Literature*, p. 137.

[2]There is an ode *to* Walter Scott in there, by one Horatio Smith, that mentions the "minstrel's lay" and "lordly *Marmion*," and there is even the text of an entire anthology that Scott edited, *Minstrelsy of the Scottish Borders*. There are 227 poems by William Bell Scott, a painter in the circle of Rossetti. But Sir Walter's own poetry, which, as Francis Jeffrey wrote in a review of the *Lay* in 1805, "has manifested a degree of genius which cannot be overlooked," was overlooked.

> Stowed away in a Montreal lumber room
> The Discobolus standeth and turneth his face to the wall

is not in the *Database*, even though it was good enough for Auden's *Oxford Book of Light Verse* and for a number of editions of *Bartlett's Familiar Quotations*. (Inexplicably, *Bartlett's* doesn't index it under "lumber" or "room" in the current edition, as it has in the past, but it is still stowed away in there.) George Meredith is listed as a mid-nineteenth-century novelist in the *New Cambridge Bibliography of English Literature* and not cross-referenced as a poet, so none of his poetry is on Chadwyck-Healey's disks, though Meredith is part of nearly every anthology of Victorian poetry. Benjamin Disraeli's blank-verse epic, called *The Revolutionary Epic*, conceived, according to *The Oxford Companion to English Literature*, as a "companion to the *Iliad*, the *Divina Commedia*, and *Paradise Lost*," was skipped over by the databasers, evidently simply because Disraeli is classed as a novelist; while five poems by his less famous father, author of *Curiosities of Literature*, made the grade, including these lines from the end of "A Defence of Poetry" addressed to James Pye, the poet laureate:

> Thou, who behold'st my Muse's rash design,
> Teach me thy art of Poetry divine;
> Or, since thy cares, alas! on me were vain,
> Teach me that harder talent—to refrain.

They make a nice table-grace for minor poets of all ages.

There are other mystifying prose-poetry juxtapositions, too. The poems that Goldsmith inserted into *The Vicar of*

Wakefield are in the *English Poetry Database* ("When lovely woman stoops to folly"), as is the "chair-lumbered closet" that Goldsmith mentions in his poem "The Haunch of Venison," but not the poems Charles Dickens put in *The Pickwick Papers* ("Creeping on, where time has been,/A rare old plant is the Ivy green"[1]), or any of Dickens's other poems or prologues:

> Awake the Present! Shall no scene display
> The tragic passion of the passing day?

Leigh Hunt's poetry is here, but not one poem by Thackeray.[2] There are eighty religious poems by a certain Francis William Newman, including the interestingly

---

[1] It was set to music several times and in song form sold tens of thousands of copies.

[2] "During almost his whole literary career he had been a sparing but an exquisite writer of a peculiar kind of verse, half serious half comic, which is scarcely inferior in excellence to his best prose," says George Saintsbury, in *A History of Nineteenth-Century Literature*. I couldn't find any *lumber* in Thackeray's poems, but I did find a good poem about a garret, called "The Garret." Here are two middle stanzas:

> Yes; 'tis a garret—let him know't who will—
>   There was my bed—full hard it was and small;
> My table there—and I decipher still
>   Half a lame couplet charcoaled on the wall.
> Ye joys, that Time hath swept with him away,
>   Come to mine eyes, ye dreams of love and fun;
> For you I pawned my watch how many a day,
>   In the brave days when I was twenty-one.
>
> And see my little Jessy, first of all;
>   She comes with pouting lips and sparkling eyes:
> Behold, how roguishly she pins her shawl

abysmal antipollution tract "Cleanliness" (1858), which staggers to its Whitmanesque peak with

> The workers of wealthy mines poison glorious mountain
>   torrents,
> Drugging them with lead or copper to save themselves petty
>   trouble;
> And the peasant groans in secret or regards it as a "landed
>   right,"
> And after some lapse of time the law counts the right valid.

The work of this Newman is included because the *New Cambridge Bibliography* lists him as a minor poet of the period 1835–1870. Not a hemistich, however, by the man's older brother, John Henry, Cardinal Newman, finds its way in, since the *New Cambridge Bibliography* categorizes Cardinal Newman as a mid-nineteenth-century prose writer. Yet Cardinal Newman's poems are both better and better known ("Lead, kindly light"); two were chosen by Francis Turner Palgrave for his *Golden Treasury, Second Series*.[1] Emily Brontë's poetry was reached by Chadwyck-Healey's rural electrification program,

---

> Across the narrow casement, curtain-wise;
> Now by the bed her petticoat glides down,
>   And when did woman look the worse in none?
> I have heard since who paid for many a gown,
>   In the brave days when I was twenty-one.

See Thackeray's *Ballads and Tales*, Scribners, 1904, pp. 103–4.

[1]It is a comfort to know, though, that two hundred and ninety of Palgrave's own poems are on these disks. Reading the poetry of people famous for their anthologies is a melancholy but instructive task.

but Charlotte's and Anne's was not, despite the fact that all three women published a book together in 1846: *Poems, by Currer, Ellis and Acton Bell*. "It stole into life," wrote Mrs. Gaskell of the book: "some weeks passed over without the mighty murmuring public discovering that three more voices were uttering their speech." It got a decent review in the *Atheneum*, and while many will concede that Emily's poetry shows the most talent, Charlotte's is not embarrassing:

> The room is quiet, thoughts alone
> People its mute tranquility;
> The yoke put off, the long task done,—
> I am, as it is bliss to be,
> Still and untroubled.
>
>   ("The Teacher's Monologue")

> Warm is the parlour atmosphere,
>   Serene the lamp's soft light;
> The vivid embers, red and clear,
>   Proclaim a frosty night.
> Books, varied, on the table lie,
>   Three children o'er them bend,
> And all, with curious, eager eye,
>   The turning leaf attend.
>
>   ("Gilbert")

And if you search the *English Poetry Database* for the words *join* and *choir* and *invisible* together you will retrieve sixty-four nineteenth-century efforts by such fixtures of the poetasters' pantheon as Atherstone, Bickersteth, Caswall, Coutts-Nevill,

Mant, Smedly, and Mary Tighe (and Byron and Keats and
Coleridge, too)—but you won't pull up George Eliot's

> O may I join the choir invisible
> Of those immortal dead who live again
> In minds made better by their presence

or any other poetry she wrote. (I found two instances of
"rubbish-heap" in Eliot's 488-page *Collected Poems*, edited
by Lucien Jenkins, but discovered no *lumber*.)

Finally, if you want to read about "hope's delusive mine"
in Samuel Johnson's verses on the death of Dr. Levet, your
hopes will be dashed; in fact if you browse for any "S. Johnson" in the database's name index you will browse in vain.
(You will find "L. Johnson," "R. Johnson," and "W. Johnson," though.) Still, the actual texts of Johnson's two best
poems, "London" and "The Vanity of Human Wishes," are
hidden within, retrievable not by poet's name but by title or
search-word, since they were republished in Dodsley's *Collection* of 1763, one of the compendia that Chadwyck-
Healey's editors (rightly) shipped off to the Philippines for
keypunching.[1] Dodsley's *Collection* fortunately also happens
to contain one version of Richard Bentley's only poem (he

---

[1] Optical scanning isn't feasible for old typefaces and foxed paper, and even
when the material is in a modern edition and hence legible to scanning software,
the raw output still demands, just as it did for the disillusioned Pope concor-
dancers in the seventies, a considerable amount of labor-intensive "markup"—
to distinguish things like titles, epigraphs, footnotes, and side-notes from text,
for instance, and stanza breaks from page breaks—not to mention the inevitable
manual fiddling afterward to fix small errors, like dashes that were read as
hyphens.

isn't listed in the name index, either), a poem itemizing the tribulations of the scholar:

> He lives inglorious, or in want,
> To college and old books confin'd;
> Instead of learn'd he's call'd pedant,
> Dunces advanc'd, he's left behind.

Samuel Johnson could recite Bentley's poem from memory, as H. W. Garrod reminds us in *Scholarship: Its Meaning and Value*, before he (Garrod, that is) goes on to praise A. E. Housman (a Bentley worshipper himself) as a "great scholar and, as I shall always think, a great poet," which is a remarkably generous assessment, since Houseman had, in a preface to his edition of Manilius,[1] viciously dismissed Garrod's earlier Manilian emendations as "singularly cheap and shallow" and judged Garrod's apparatus criticus "often defective and sometimes visibly so."

Housman would probably say similarly rude things about the holes, minor and major, in the *English Poetry Database* (no Jonathan Swift at all, anywhere?[2]) since Housman spent

---

[1]Manilius being the Roman astrological poet who gave Johnson the tag he applied to Cowley and the rest of the Metaphysicals, *discordia concors* (not to be confused with Horace's *concordia discors*, or Gratian's *Concordia discordantium canonum*): you can find the Manilian reference in a footnote to the life of Cowley in G. Birkbeck Hill's 1905 edition of Johnson's *Lives of the Poets*, a lovely example of old-fashioned scholarship, or you can search the Saturnian rings of the Latin CD-ROM published by the Packard Humanities Institute and Silver Mountain Software, which takes about five minutes.

[2]No Macaulay's *Lays of Ancient Rome*? Only one of Daniel Defoe's poems? Nothing by Lewis Theobald?

most of his life absorbed in "those minute and pedantic studies in which I am fitted to excel and which give me pleasure," and was intolerant of grand schemes and mechanized shortcuts. Moreover, his own 1896 volume, *A Shropshire Lad*, is missing from the disks, possibly for copyright reasons, a fact that would have nettled him, although he would have pretended not to care.

But we, on the other hand, shouldn't say rude things. This database may be, as John Sutherland pointed out in the *London Review of Books* (vol. 16, no. 11, 9 June 1994), the most significant development in literary scholarship since xerography. And even Sutherland's high praise is insufficient. The *EPFTD*, as some refer to it, is a mind-manuring marvel, and we are lucky that a lot is left out (provided that no university libraries, tempted by its aura of comprehensiveness, "withdraw"—which is to say, get rid of—the unelectrified source books themselves); we don't want every corner of poetry lit with the same even, bright light, for such a uniformity would interfere with what Housman himself called the "hide-and-seek" of learning. The god of scholars, Housman pointed out in his "Introductory Lecture," "planted in us the desire to find out what is concealed, and stored the universe with hidden things that we might delight ourselves in discovering them." And the fact is that Chadwyck-Healey's demiurgic project comes so much closer than anything else in paper or plastic to the unattainable *om* of total inclusion (containing, by my estimate, several thousand times more poetry than *Great Poetry Classics*, itself a fine shovelware CD-ROM published by World Library, Inc.) that hunter-gatherers of all predilections can pretend, some of the time, when it calms their research anxieties to do so, that no obscurity of consequence will be left unfingered. After all, the disks hold (on top of hymns before 1800, and nursery rhymes) many verse *translations* from other languages into English, if they were published before 1800—a very useful subcategory for the lumber-struck.

The British Library's newspaper collection occupies several buildings in Colindale, north of London, near a former Royal Air Force base that is now a museum of aviation. On October 20, 1940, a German airplane—possibly mistaking the library complex for an aircraft-manufacturing plant—dropped a bomb on it. Ten thousand volumes of Irish and English papers were destroyed; fifteen thousand more were damaged. Unscathed, however, was a very large foreign-newspaper collection, including many American titles: thousands of fifteen-pound brick-thick folios bound in marbled boards, their pages stamped in red with the British Museum's crown-and-lion symbol of curatorial responsibility.

Bombs spared the American papers, but recent managerial policy has not—most were sold off in a blind auction in the fall of 1999. One of the library's treasures was a seventy-year run, in about eight hundred volumes, of Joseph Pulitzer's exuberantly polychromatic newspaper, the New York *World*. Pulitzer discovered that illustrations sold the news; in the 1890s, he began printing four-color Sunday supplements and splash-panel cartoons. The more maps, murder-scene diagrams, ultra-wide front-page political cartoons, fashion sketches, needlepoint patterns, children's puzzles, and comics that Pulitzer published, the higher the *World*'s sales climbed; by the mid-nineties, its circulation was the largest of any paper in the country. William Randolph Hearst moved to New York in 1895 and copied Pulitzer's innovations and poached his staff, and the war between the two men created modern privacy-probing, muckraking, glamour-smitten journalism. A million people a day once read Pulitzer's *World*; now an original set is a good deal rarer than a Shakespeare First Folio or the Gutenberg Bible.

Besides the *World*, the British Library also possessed one of the last sweeping runs of the sumptuous *Chicago Tribune*—about 1,300 volumes, reaching from 1888 to 1958, complete with bonus four-color art supplements on heavy stock from the 1890s ("This Paper is Not Complete Without the Color Illustration" says the box on the masthead); extravagant layouts of illustrated fiction; elaborately hand-lettered ornamental headlines; and decades of page-one political cartoons by John T. McCutcheon. The British Library owned, as well, an enormous set of the *San Francisco Chronicle* (one of perhaps two that are left, the second owned by the Chronicle Publishing Company itself and inaccessible to scholars), which in its heyday was filled with gorgeously drippy art-nouveau graphics. And the library owned a monster accumulation of what one could argue is the best newspaper in U.S. history, the New York *Herald Tribune*, along with its two tributaries, Horace Greeley's anti-slavery *Tribune* and James Gordon Bennett's initially pro-slavery *Herald*.

The *Herald Tribune* set carries all the way through to 1966, when the paper itself died—it, too, may be the last surviving long run anywhere. And there was a goodly stretch of *The New York Times* on the British Library's shelves (1915 through 1958), with Al Hirschfeld drawings and hundreds of luminously fine-grained, sepia-tinted "Rotogravure Picture Sections" bound in place.

All these newspapers have been very well cared for over the years—the volumes I was allowed to examine in September 1999 were in lovely shape. The pictorial sections, but for their unfamiliar turn-of-the-century artwork, looked and felt as if they had peeled off a Hoe cylinder press day before yesterday.

But then, wood-pulp newspapers of fifty and a hundred years ago are, contrary to incessant library propaganda, often surprisingly well preserved. Everyone knows that newsprint, if left in the sun, quickly turns yellow and brittle (a connective wood ingredient called lignin, which newsprint contains in abundance, reacts with sunlight), but rolls of microfilm— and floppies and DVDs—don't do well in the sun, either; so far, many of the old volumes seem to be doing a better job of holding their original images than the miniature plastic reproductions of them that libraries have seen fit to put in their places over the years. Binding is very important. The stitching together of fifteen (or thirty or sixty) single issues of a paper into one large, heavy book does much to keep the sheets sound; the margins often become brown and flaky, since moist, warm air reacts with the acidic compounds in the paper and weakens it, and the binding glues can stop working; but a little deeper inside the flatland of the tightly closed folio, the sheer weight of the text-block squeezes out most of the air. The effect is roughly equivalent to vacuum-sealing the inner expanses of the pages: the paper suffers much less impairment as a result.

Many librarians, however, have managed to convince themselves, and us, that if a newspaper was printed after 1870 or so, it will inevitably self-destruct or "turn to dust" any minute, soon, in a matter of a few years—1870 being the all-important date after which, in American newsprint mills, papermaking pulps consisting of cooked rags gradually began to give way to pulps made of stone-ground wood. But "soon" is a meaningless word in the context of a substance with a life as long as that of the printed page—indeed, it is a word that allows for all sorts of abuses. Early on, fledgling microfilm companies fed the fear of impermanence with confident mispredictions. Charles Z. Case, an executive at Recordak, Kodak's microfilm subsidiary, wrote in 1936: "Since the adoption of wood-sulphite paper for newspaper printing, a newspaper file has had a life of from 5 to 40 years depending on the quality of the paper, the conditions of storage, and the degree of use." Had Case's forecast held true, the volume of the *Chicago Tribune* for July 1911 that lies open before me as I type (to an influenza-inspired illustrated section on "A New Theory of Baby Rearing") would have expired at least half a century ago. Thomas Martin, chief of the manuscript division of the Library of Congress in the thirties, agreed with the Recordak salesman: "Old wood-pulp files which have only a few years' duration remaining in them should be photographed on film as soon as satisfactory results can be obtained. In such cases we really have no choice but to make or take film copies, the original will soon crumble into dust."

But the originals didn't crumble into dust. Keyes Metcalf, a microfilm pioneer and the director of the libraries at Harvard, in 1941 predicted that the "total space requirements" of research libraries "will be reduced by paper disintegration." Then five, ten, twenty years went by, and the paper—even the supposedly ephemeral newsprint—was still there. So librarians began getting rid of it anyway. If you destroy the physical evidence, nobody will know how skewed your predictions were.

Vilified though it may be, ground-wood pulp is one of the great inventions of the late nineteenth century: it gave us cheap paper, and cheap paper transformed the news. "All that it is necessary for a man to do on going into a paper-mill is to take off his shirt, hand it to the devil who officiates at one extremity, and have it come out 'Robinson Crusoe' at the other," wrote the founder of the New York *Sun* in 1837. But there were never enough shirts, and in 1854 rag shortages lifted the price of newsprint to alarming heights. The arrival of the brothers Pagenstecher, who in the 1860s imported a German machine that shredded logs to pulp by jamming their ends against a circular, water-cooled grinding stone, brought prices way down—from twelve cents a pound in 1870, to seven cents a pound in 1880, to less than two cents a pound in 1900. The drop gave Pulitzer and Hearst the plentiful page space to sell big ads, and allowed their creations to flower into the gaudy painted ladies they had become by the first decade of the twentieth century.

There's no question that wood pulps are in general weaker than rag pulps; and old newsprint, especially, tears easily, and it can become exceedingly fragile if it is stored, say, on the cement floor of a library basement, near heating pipes, for a few decades. But the degree of fragility varies from title to title and run to run, and many fragile things (old quilts, old clocks, astrolabes, dried botanical specimens, Egyptian glass, daguerreotypes, early computers) are deemed worth pre-serving despite, or even because of, their fragility. The most delicate volume I've come across (a month of the Detroit *Evening News* from 1892), though the pages were mostly detached, and though it shed flurries of marginal flakes when I moved it around, could nonetheless be page-turned and read with a modicum of care—there was an interesting article, with two accompanying etchings, about a city shel-ter for "homeless wanderers." (Sinners slept on wooden bunks without bedding, while the newly converted got cots with mattresses, and a reading room.)

Old newsprint is very acidic—and so? Our agitation over the acid in paper is not rational. Just because a given page has a low pH (a pH of 7 is neutral, below that is acidic) doesn't mean that it can't be read. There are five-hundred-year-old book papers that remain strong and flexible despite pH lev-els under five, a fact which has led one conservation scien-tist to conclude that "the acidity of the paper alone is not necessarily indicative of the state of permanence of paper." It is difficult, in fact, to get a meaningful measure of how alkaline or acidic a paper actually is, since chemicals on the surface behave differently than those held within; the stan-dard scientific tests (which often rely on a blender) don't discriminate. It's true that, all things being equal, pH-neutral paper seems to keep its properties longer than paper that is made with acid-containing or acid-forming additives; scientists have been making this observation, on and off, for more than eighty years. But saying that one substance is stronger than another is not the same as saying that the weaker substance is on the verge of self-destruction. A stainless-steel chair may be more durable than a wooden one, but the wooden one isn't necessarily going to collapse the next time you take a seat.

Can't scientists foretell with a fair degree of certainty how long a newspaper collection of a given age will last? No, they can't; there has never been a long-term study that attempted to plot an actual loss-of-strength curve for samples of naturally aging newsprint, or indeed for samples of any paper. Years ago, William K. Wilson, a paper scientist, began such a study at the National Bureau of Standards. For three decades he recorded the degradative changes undergone by a set of commercial book papers; then somebody decided to clean out the green filing cabinet in which the papers were stored—end of experiment. "That raised my blood pressure a little," Wilson told me.

In the absence of real long-term data, predictions have relied on methodologically shaky "artificial aging" (or "accelerated aging") experiments, in which you bake a paper sample in a laboratory oven for a week or two and then belabor it with standardized tests. With your test results in hand, you can, by applying a bit of chemist's legerdemain called the Arrhenius equation, come up with what appears be a reasonable estimate of the number of years the sample will last at shirtsleeve temperatures. But the results of these sorts of divinatory calculations, invoked with head-shaking gravity by library administrators, have been uniformly wrong, and they are now viewed with skepticism by many paper scientists. The authors of the *ASTM Standards*, for example, write that the use of the Arrhenius equation to predict the life expectancy of paper is "an interesting academic exercise, but the uncertainty of extrapolation is too great for this approach to be taken very seriously"; William Wilson points out that you can't predict how long an egg will last in the carton by putting it in boiling water for five minutes. Paper has a complex and as yet ill-charted chemistry, with many different molecular and mechanical processes under way concurrently; one Swedish researcher wrote that it is a "naïve hope" to think that we can estimate "the life length of books by means of accelerated aging tests and [the] Arrhenius approach."

In a way, however, all surviving newspaper collections, in and out of libraries, are taking part in an immense self-guided experiment in natural aging—an experiment that confutes the doctrine of newsprint's imminent disintegration. Peter Waters, former head of the conservation lab at the Library of Congress, told me that he sees no reason why old ground-wood pulp paper can't hold its textual freight for "a hell of a long time" if it is properly stored. He notes that most of the cellulose-sundering chemical reactions that can happen to a book or newspaper volume seem to take place in the first decade or so of its life; fifty years of handling paper (Waters is a master bookbinder) have taught him that the rate at which paper loses strength decreases signifi-

cantly over time—the curve of observed decay levels out.
There is a very good chance, then, that a volume of the New
York *World* that is doing okay at age ninety will be in pretty
much the same shape when it is a hundred and eighty, assum-
ing someone is willing to take decent care of it.

The British Library's papers had escaped the Blitz and the
agenbite of their own acidity, but their keepers craved the
space they occupied. English law requires that the library
preserve British newspapers in the original but makes no
such stipulation for foreign papers, and in 1996 the library
quietly announced its intent to rid itself of about sixty
thousand volumes—almost all the non-Commonwealth
papers printed after 1850 for which they had bought microfilm copies. (The microfilm, much of it shot in the United
States decades ago, is of varying quality—some good, some
not good, all on high-contrast black-and-white stock,
which wasn't designed to reproduce the intermediate shades
of photographs.) The announcement appeared as an inside
article in the newspaper library's newsletter; it was written
up not long after as a short wire-service story— "British
Library Giving Away Historic Newspapers."

In 1997 the library selected for discard more than seventy-
five runs of Western European papers and periodicals, from
France, Belgium, Germany, Austria, Greece, Italy, Portugal,
Spain, the Netherlands, and Switzerland. They were able to
place a number of these titles with national and university
libraries; others they planned to sell or throw away. (I first
found out about these developments in 1999; library offi-
cials still have not provided an accounting of where everything went.) Baylor University in Texas asked for, and got,

eight runs of important French and Italian papers from the 1850s on, some of which will become part of their renowned Armstrong Browning collection, since Robert and Elizabeth Barrett Browning likely would have read those papers in their expatriate years.

Very few people knew any of this was going on. Although I interviewed a number of American newspaper librarians and dealers, I heard nothing of it; and even well-connected heads of libraries within England—such as David McKitterick, librarian of Trinity College, Cambridge, who serves on an advisory board of the British Library—were not informed of the "overseas disposals project," and learned of it only late in 1999, when word began to get out. McKitterick objects to the "very quiet way" in which the deaccessioning was handled (at the very least, other British libraries should have had a better-advertised chance at the papers, he says), and he is troubled by what is on the lists; he mentions, for instance, the newspapers of pre–Revolutionary Russia, Nazi Germany, and occupied France. "I've now talked to a number of scholars about this," McKitterick told me, "and they're absolutely furious. When you replace a broadsheet newspaper with microfilm, you effectively kill stone dead much of what it meant at its time. Film can't deal adequately with illustrations—and yet they were discarding the great French illustrated papers of the early twentieth century."

But library administrators had other things to think about than illustration and scholarship. "Increasing pressure on the storage facilities at the Colindale site" was the justification for their desperate act. One of the finest libraries in the world was unable or unwilling to buy, build, retrofit, or lease a ten-thousand-square-foot warehouse anywhere in England that could hold their unique international collection.

With Western Europe taken care of, having freed up thousands of linear meters of shelf space without any political trouble, the British Library then moved on to papers from Eastern Europe, South America, and the USA. They sent out notices of availability to the Library of Congress and the American Antiquarian Society, of Worcester, Massachusetts. The Library of Congress rejected everything, but the American Antiquarian Society, which owns a famous collection of early papers (bound in black with gold trim), took several titles, mainly covering the era of the Civil War and immediately afterward. "The redcoats are coming!" librarians there said, shelving the red-spined British volumes next to their black ones. Richard Bland College in Petersburg, Virginia, claimed several nineteenth-century runs. John Blair, head of the history department, says he would have taken more of the British Library's collection if his college had had more space; Blair remembers working as a stock boy in a large Massachusetts library in the fifties and hauling home dozens of unwanted newspaper volumes. "They just junked them," he said; he has used them for years in his classes. Blair likened the clearing out of newspaper collections to the overeager tearing up of track as the railroads went into decline. "Now maybe they regret losing some of those rights-of-way," he said.

No other libraries expressed interest in the huge remaining mass of U.S. material. The plan, blessed by the British Library's board, was to offer to dealers whatever libraries left unclaimed; anything dealers didn't want was to be thrown away: "Material for which we cannot find a home will be offered to dealers for sale, or as a last resort sent for pulping." Brian Lang, the director of the British Library, reiterated this plan in a letter to me: "The intention is that runs of newspapers for which no bids have been received will be pulped."

Chapter Two
ORIGINAL KEEPSAKES
from DOUBLE FOLD

I didn't want the newspapers to be dispersed by dealers or "pulped" (awful word), so I hastily formed a non-profit corporation called the American Newspaper Repository, and, when it was clear that the auction was going to go forward whether I liked it or not, I submitted bids. A dealer from Williamsport, Pennsylvania, Timothy Hughes Rare and Early Newspapers, also bid on the papers, as it turned out. Hughes owns a medium-sized, pale blue warehouse, tidily kept, filled with rows of industrial shelving; on the shelves rest about eighteen thousand newspaper volumes. He is an undemonstrative man with a small mustache, honest in his business dealings, who was formerly on the board of the Little League Museum in South Williamsport. His usual practice is to "disbind" the newspapers—that is, cut them out of their chronological context with a utility knife (you can hear the binding strings pop softly as the blade travels down the inner gutter of the volume)—and sell the eye-catching headline issues (Al Capone, the *Lusitania*, Bonnie and Clyde, Amelia Earhart) or issues containing primordial Coke ads or Thomas

Nast illustrations, shrink-wrapped against white cardboard, at paper shows (where buyers gather to look over vintage postcards, baseball cards, posters, and other ephemera) or through his printed catalog or website. His father, jolly and self-effacing, is a retired sharpener of band-saw blades, as was his grandfather; now his father and his brother, along with an amiable ex-schoolteacher named Marc, are employees of the company, filling orders, moving pallets of incoming volumes around with a forklift, writing catalog copy, and gradually working down the inventory, almost all of which came from libraries.

If American libraries had been doing the job we paid them to do, and innocently trusted that they were doing, over the past five decades—if they had been taking reasonable care of our communal newspaper collections rather than stacking them in all the wrong places, and finally selling them to book-breakers or dumping them in the trash outright (an employee of one Southern library recently rescued from a Dumpster, and successfully resold to a dealer, a run of *Harper's Weekly* worth ten thousand dollars)—then the British Library's decision to auction off millions of pages of urban life, although it would mark a low point of cultural husbandry, would not have been such a potentially disastrous loss to future historians. Fifty years ago, after all, there were bound sets, even double sets, of all the major metropolitan dailies safely stored in libraries around the United States.

But that is no longer true. The Library of Congress and the New York Public Library once owned Pulitzer's New York *World* complete, for instance, and Harvard University, the University of Chicago, the Chicago Public Library, and the Chicago Tribune Company once owned sets of the *Chicago Tribune*. They don't now. ("I'm sorry to say and appalled to say that they were tossed," an employee of the reference department of the *Chicago Tribune* said to me. "It was before my time.") At Columbia University (whose school of journalism Pulitzer founded), at the New York Public Library, and at the Library of Congress, you can flip through memoirs, biographies, scholarly studies, and original holograph letters of Joseph Pulitzer, works that describe his innovations in graphic design and recount his public squabble with Hearst over *The Yellow Kid*, a popular color cartoon that first appeared in the *World* in the 1890s—a squabble that begat the term "yellow journalism." But the *World* itself, the half-million-page masterpiece in the service of which Pulitzer stormed and swore and finally went blind, was slapdashedly microfilmed in monochrome and thrown out by the New York Public Library, probably in the early fifties. Columbia said good-bye to its *World* at some point thereafter; the New-York Historical Society did so around 1990. The University of Chicago library, under the direction of micro-madman Herman Fussler (former lead librarian and information specialist for the Manhattan Project), produced a bad copy of the *Chicago Tribune* in the fifties as well. The Library of Congress was quick to clear its shelves of the *World* and most of the *Chicago Tribune* and replace them with copies of the NYPL's and the University of Chicago's microfilm; and copies of that very same mid-century microfilm— edge-blurred, dark, gappy, with text cut off of some pages, faded to the point of illegibility on others—will now have to serve for patrons of the British Library, too.

All the major newspaper repositories—the Center for Research Libraries in Chicago, for instance, and the State Historical Society of Wisconsin, both of which once had collections of national importance—have long since bet the farm on film and given away, sold, or thrown out most of their original volumes published after 1880 or so. Nearly all major university libraries, state libraries, and large public libraries have done the same. Even the great American Antiquarian Society, having decided some years ago to narrow its focus to publications before 1876, is arranging with Timothy Hughes to swap long runs of some small-town papers—the Fitchburg (Massachusetts) *Sentinel* from 1888 on, for example—for older titles that they want.

The Kansas State Historical Society, founded by a group of newspaper editors in 1875, had, until a few years ago, an unusually fine out-of-state newspaper assemblage, including a pre-Civil War file of the New York *Tribune*, a long run of the Boston *Investigator*, and a large number of otherwise impossible-to-find Western and territorial papers. Then the society put up a new building that was smaller than it should have been and, in 1997, had an auction. One observer told me that the lots that Kansas ended up selling were so unusual, so valuable, that a group of buyers got together ahead of time to divvy things up, so that the bidding wouldn't go completely insane. It was "once-in-a-lifetime stuff," this observer said. The next step, according to Patricia Michaelis, the director of the library and archives division, was to dispose of most of the society's comprehensive collection of original Kansas papers printed after 1875, offering them first to institutions and then throwing out the leavings. Michaelis believes that the original papers are doomed anyway: "They're just inherently going to crumble apart, no matter what you do to them, because of the acid content." About half of the people who use the library come for the newspaper collection. Do they like the microfilm? Michaelis laughed. "Well, it's the only option we give them."

At another midwestern historical society, out in a pole barn, a collection was stacked twelve feet high and twenty feet wide near rows of shaft-drive bicycles and the disassembled pieces of a nineteenth-century machine shop. There were thousands of volumes of local papers and a run of *The New York Times*. Shawn Godwin, an employee of the society at the time, wrote me that this "cube of history" was made to disappear by order of the head archivist: the volumes were chainsawed in half and fed into the steam engine that powered a vintage sawmill exhibit. "I asked one of the more sympathetic assistant directors if it would be possible to sneak a few of the volumes away," Godwin writes. "He indicated if I was discreet and did not make a big deal about it it might be okay." Godwin saved a small stack and tried to avoid looking at the column of smoke rising from the sawmill.

The cleanout continues. Since the mid-eighties, the vast U.S. Newspaper Program, a government project whose aims are to catalog as many newspapers in the country as possible (a worthy goal) and to microfilm those local papers that were passed over in earlier decades, has given libraries about forty-five million dollars in so-called preservation money—

and zero dollars for storage space. The National Endowment for the Humanities, which pays for the U.S. Newspaper Program (and funds a related enterprise, the Brittle Books Program), makes no requirement that libraries actually preserve, in the physical sense of "reshelve," their originals after they have been sent out for federally funded filming. The effect of all this NEH microfilm money has been to trigger a last huge surge of discarding, as libraries use federal preservation grants to solve their local space problems. Not since the monk-harassments of sixteenth-century England has a government tolerated, indeed stimulated, the methodical eradication of so much primary-source material.

Surely this material is all available on the Web by now, or will be soon? In time, eighty or a hundred years of a great urban paper could well become the source for a historical database of richness and utility. But at the moment, the scanning and storing and indexing of hundreds of thousands of pages of tiny type, along with halftone photos and color illustrations, would be a fearsomely expensive job; and even if money were limitless, there would remain the formidable technical challenge of achieving acceptable levels of resolution using digital cameras for formats as large as those of a newspaper spread. Nor will high-quality digital facsimiles of our major papers ever exist unless we decide right now to do a much better job of holding on to the originals—even the mangy ones with crumbly edges. You can't digitize something that has been sold off piecemeal or thrown away, after all; and attempts to scan the page-images of newspapers from old microfilm have not worked well—and will never work well—because the microfilm itself is often at the squint-to-make-it-out level. HarpWeek, a venture that offers a digital copy of *Harper's Weekly* on the Web, spent tens of thousands of dollars trying to scan the available microfilm, but they found that thirty percent of the resultant images were bad. Now they're working from two original sets of the journal, both of which they've cut out of their bindings in order to set the loose pages flat on the scanner.

Amid the general devastation, there are some librarians of courage and foresight whose accomplishments are as yet unsung. The Boston Public Library, owing to the belief of Charles Longley—the recently retired curator of microtexts and newspapers—that his institution's accumulated newspaper files are "part of the City's own heritage and the Library would be remiss in not retaining them," not only has held on to all its existing collections but has continued to lay away all the recent output of Boston and selected Massachusetts papers, wrapped in brown paper, right up through the present; and the library has taken ownership of important sets of bound Boston newspapers once owned by Harvard and other libraries in the region as well. Longley was lucky: his views were shared by the city's longtime librarian, the late Philip McNiff; often a change of administration proves fatal to a great collection.

At Ohio State, a librarian named Lucy Caswell, who wears quiet silk scarves and directs the Cartoon Research Library, is almost single-handedly attempting to rebuild a bound-volume collection of national scope—buying back for scholarly use material offered by dealers and collectors, most notably the lifetime harvest of Bill Blackbeard and his San Francisco Academy of Comic Art.

Several years ago, Caswell bought some volumes of the *Chicago Tribune* (from a dealer, who bought them from another dealer); two of them, one from 1899 and one from 1914, were out on a trolley at the Cartoon Research Library when I visited—four-inch-thick buckram-backed bulwarks, with heavy pull-straps triple-riveted to the binding in order to assist the frowning researcher in hauling their massiveness from the shelf. Their exteriors are scuffed and battered, but they are things of beauty nonetheless; they made me think of Mickey's book of broom-awakening spells in *Fantasia*. I opened the volume from 1914. The inside boards displayed the seal of Harvard University, and below it I read:

FROM THE BEQUEST OF

ICHABOD TUCKER

[Class of 1791]

OF SALEM, MASS.

The paper wasn't crumbling—it was easily turned and read. I called Harvard's microform department and asked if they had the *Chicago Tribune* on paper from 1899 and 1914, just to be sure that the Ohio volumes weren't from a duplicate set that they had sold. A sincere-sounding reference woman in the microforms department said, "Oh, we would never have hard copies going back that far—they just don't keep." They don't keep, kiddo, if you don't keep them.

Aside from what Lucy Caswell and Charles Longley have been able to save, the annihilation of once accessible collections of major daily papers of the late nineteenth and twentieth centuries is pretty close to total. Some state libraries—Pennsylvania's, for instance, in Harrisburg—reached back further than the 1870s or 1880s as they designed their disposal programs, and used 1850 as a draconian dump-after date. "Pennsylvania was the first state to undertake statewide microfilming and destruction of its newspaper files," Bill Blackbeard told me. "They did an extraordinarily, brutally thorough job of it. Unfortunately, some of the earliest color Sunday comic strips were printed in Philadelphia newspapers. So I never have gotten to see very many of those." The State Library of Pennsylvania did not keep its original bound set of *The Philadelphia Inquirer*, and neither did the Free Library of Philadelphia—a librarian there wrote me that wood-pulp newsprint "falls apart." Bell and Howell Information and Learning (formerly University Microfilms) will, however, sell the whole *Inquirer* to you on spools of archival polyester, encased in little white cardboard boxes, for $621,515.

Bell and Howell/UMI now owns microfilm negatives for most of the big papers in the country; and, to the extent that there are no originals left to scan when scanning resolution improves, its "master" microfilm (some of it inherited from now defunct filming labs and of poor quality) will perforce become the basis for any future digital versions of old newspapers, access to which the company will also control. Bell and Howell has successfully privatized our past: whether we like it or not, they possess a near monopoly on the reproduction rights for the chief primary sources of twentieth-century history.

Where did all the spurned papers go? Many were thrown out—and continue to be thrown out as statewide filming projects progress—but a colossal residue rests at a company called Historic Newspaper Archives, Inc., the biggest name in the birth-date business. If you call Hammacher Schlemmer, say, or Potpourri, or the Miles Kimball catalog, to order an "original keepsake newspaper" from the day a loved one was born, Historic Newspaper Archives will fill your order. In the company's twenty-five thousand square feet of warehouse space in Rahway, New Jersey, innumerable partially gutted volumes wait in lugubrious disorder on tall industrial shelves and stacked in four-foot piles and on pallets. I paid a visit one winter afternoon. The Christmas rush was over, and the place was very quiet. Torn sheets, sticking out from damaged volumes overhead, slapped and fluttered in a warm breeze that came from refrigerator-sized heaters mounted on the ceiling. When an order came in for a particular date, a worker would pull out a volume of the Lewiston *Evening Journal*, say (once of Bowdoin College), slice out the issue, neaten the rough edges using a large electric machine called a guillotine (adorned on one side with photos of swimsuit models), and slip it in a clear vinyl sleeve for shipping. Every order comes with a "certificate of authenticity" printed in florid script.

Not everything was on shelves—some were piled three pallets high against the wall; and the University of Maryland's large collection, a recent arrival, occupied about a thousand square feet of floor near the loading dock. The *Herald Tribune* set that the Historic Newspaper Archive is gradually dismembering is bound in pale-blue cloth and is in very good condition (where it hasn't gone under the knife, that is); its bookplates announce that it was the gift of Mrs. Ogden Reid, who owned and ran the *Tribune*, more or less, in the forties and fifties. It is a multi-edition file: five editions for each day are separately bound. I would guess that this was at one time the *Herald Tribune*'s own corporate-historical set; Mrs. Reid no doubt believed that she was ensuring its careful continuance by donating it to a library. Hy Gordon, the no-nonsense general manager of the archives, told me that he believes he got his *Herald Tribune*s from the New York Public Library. Gordon sold me one volume from the set, for February 1–15, 1934 (including rotogravure sections and color cartoons by Rea Irwin) at a discounted price of three hundred dollars plus shipping.

(The NYPL divested themselves of their *Tribune* run, but it must be commended for keeping a huge cobbled-together set of *The New York Times*, from 1851 right up through 1985, several decades of which exist in a special rag-paper library edition. They will let you read from it in room 315, where they serve "semi-rare" material under supervision. The run has some gaping holes—for instance, there are no volumes at all for the years from 1915 through 1925. And no research library, I believe, has saved the *Times* in paper over the past decade: the paper now prints thousands of color photographs a year, but you wouldn't know that from the film.)

I told Hy Gordon that I thought some librarians had exaggerated the severity of newsprint's deterioration. "Oh yeah, yeah, it doesn't fall apart," he agreed. "The ends might crack, but that's all. The newspaper's still fine."

I said I was distressed that so many libraries were getting rid of their bound newspapers.

"Don't be distressed," he said. "There are a lot of things more important in life."

Are there really? More important than the fact that this country has strip-mined a hundred and twenty years of its history? I'm not so sure. The Historic Newspaper Archives owns what is now probably the largest "collection" of post-1880 U.S. papers anywhere in the country, or the world, for that matter—a ghastly anti-library. They own it in order to destroy it. "Here are rare and original newspapers with assured value many from the Library of Congress," says the Archives' sales brochure—all for sale for $39.50 an issue. I saw identifying bookplates or spine-markings from the New York State Library, the New York Public Library, Brown University, the San Francisco Public Library, Yale, the Wisconsin Historical Society Library, the American Antiquarian Society, and many others. A now mutilated run of the New York *World* has this bookplate:

Presented to

THE NEW-YORK HISTORICAL SOCIETY

by

THOMAS W. DEWART

former President of The Sun

and by

ROY W. HOWARD

President and Editor of the

New York World-Telegram and The Sun

And there was a shelf of volumes bearing this warning:

THESE FILES ARE FOR
PERMANENT RECORD OF

The St. Louis Republic

HANDLE WITH CARE
Positively Must Not be Cut
or Clipped

The warning has not been heeded.

Chapter Five
from A BOX OF MATCHES

Good morning, it's 4:20 a.m.—You know, I used to have trouble sleeping, but now I have much less trouble because I'm getting up at four in the morning. Before five, anyway. I'm so sleepy that I sleep well. For some years I relied on suicidal thoughts to help me go to sleep. By day I'm not a particularly morbid person, but at night I would lie in bed imagining that I was hammering a knitting needle into my ear, or swan-diving off a ledge into a black void at the bottom of which were a dozen sharp, slippery stalagmites. Wearing a helmet and pilot's gear, I would miniaturize myself, and wait for a giant screwdriver to unscrew the hatch at the nose of a bullet. I would be lowered into the control room of the bullet, whereupon the hatch would be screwed tight over me. At a certain moment, I would flick a switch and the gun would fire, throwing me back in my seat. I would shoot out the muzzle and over the sleeping city, following a path towards my own house; I would crash through the window and plunge toward my own head, and when the bullet dove into my brain I would fall asleep.

Now I lie in bed and think a few random things about soil

erosion or painting a long yellow strip on the side of a black ship, and because I've gotten up so early, I just fall asleep. The soporific suicidalism peaked several years ago, when we were staying for a few months in San Diego, so that I could "encourage" a group of doctors who were supposed to be revising their textbook. My brain was alive with the night-crawlerly unfinishedness of the project, and there were four palm trees that I could see from the window of the room that I was using as a temporary office. The palms were beautiful trees in their way, especially as part of a quartet, but there is an intrinsic scrawniness to the palm, which grows like a flaring match, with a little fizzle of green at the top. It is doing only what is absolutely necessary to do to be a tree; and it has big, coarse leaves—intemperate leaves—and the bark shows its years on the outside, so that the tree has no secrets: it doesn't have to die and be cut down before you can date its birth. I would look up at those four trees as I worked, and then at night I would imagine digging my own grave, because it just seemed that it would be so much easier to die than to get those three contentious doctors to contribute their material for the new and heavily revised edition of *Spinal Cord Trauma*. Claire and the children would be fully provided for as long as I was able to craft a way of dying that didn't seem like suicide. But eventually the new edition was written, and then it was copyedited and indexed and published and distributed, and now medical-school students are buying it and underlining things in it, and all is as it should be.

At around four thirty, sometimes later, the freight-train whistle goes off. At seven I have to get dressed and drop my daughter Phoebe off at school and drive to work. I would like to visit the factory that makes train horns, and ask them how they are able to arrive at that chord of eternal mournfulness. Is it deliberately sad? Are the horns saying, Be careful, stay away from this train or it will run you over and then people will grieve, and their grief will be as the inconsolable wail of this horn through the night? The out-of-tuneness of the triad is part of its beauty. A hundred years ago, a trolley line and two passenger trains came through this town; Rudyard Kipling reportedly stayed here for a week on his way inland to his house in Vermont, where he wrote the *Just So Stories*. "How the Leopard Got His Spots" is a good one. My mother read it to my brother and me, and it changed the way I thought about shadows. There were several places in our yard that offered Kipling's kind of jigsawed shade. The euonymus tree that grew near the edge of our property worked best. Euonymus bark has beautiful fins, and under this low tree I could sit and watch the sunlight break into pieces.

I like deciduous trees, frankly, especially trees with lichen growing on them. I like living in the east, I like old brass boxes with scratches, I like the way fireplaces look when they've held thousands of fires. The fireplace that I'm sitting in front of was built, supposedly, in 1780. How many fires has it held? Two hundred a year times two hundred years: forty thousand fires? I like to burn wood. I've only discovered this recently. Last year, Claire gave me an ax for my birthday, and I began using it to chop up the scrap wood that the contractors piled up where they were reconstructing our slumped barn. If you bring the ax down really hard, right in the middle of a six-inch board, the board will break

in two longways, and the grain of the breakage will sometimes detour nicely around a knothole. Then you can chop
across the grain. Apple boughs are very hard to chop, even
the old gray ones that have lost their bark. You slam away at
them for five minutes and then suddenly, if you hit them
just right, they leap up at you and whack you in the face.
Contractor's scraps burn with many little explosions and
whistling sighs.

When we had burned through most of the scraps, I called
up a wood man and ordered a cord. A cord is a unit of measure that means "a goodly amount." The wood man used a
large pincering hook to snag the quartered logs off his
truck. He drove off with a pale blue check in his hand, leaving us with a heap of logs. This heap Claire and I, over the
next week, built into a long, neat edifice against the barn.
You crisscross the logs: three one way, and then three over
those going the other way, and you put each crisscrossing
pile next to the other, and you have to choose the logs so
that the pile will remain stable and not topple; and you sur-
mount the whole architecture with a roof made of stray
pieces of bark. It takes on an air of permanency, like a stone
wall—so finished seeming that you hesitate before pulling
from it the first few logs for burning.

The woodpile quickly became an object of fascination
for the duck. She roots in between the logs and bangs at the
bark with her beak until some breaks off, to see if there are
bugs underneath. Now that everything is frozen, there is
much less for her to eat there, but once in the fall I lifted a
bottom log for her and she found an ant colony and several
worms which she consumed with much lusty beak smack-

ing. She is a dirty eater. She snuffles in mud and grass and then goes over to the plastic wading pool that we set up for her and drinks from it, and streams of dirt flow from her beak as she scoops up the water. When she has found a patch of wet earth or weeds that particularly pleases, she makes a whimpering sound of happiness, as a piglet would at the udder. I had no idea that ducks were capable of such noises. In coloration she resembles a tabby cat.

The other day I pried up a log from the stiff ground and turned it over so that Greta (that's the duck's name) could have a once-over on it before I brought it inside. It's not just that I want to give her a treat; it's also that I don't want to be bringing termites or strange larvae into the house. She rooted all over the exposed underside, as if she were Tele-typing a wire-service story on it. Finally she located, hidden in a crevice, a brown thing that excited her. She was able to pry it out: it was a frozen slug. Its slime had grown ice crys-tals, giving it a kind of fur. I couldn't tell if it was hibernat-ing or dead. The duck tumbled it around in her beak and tossed it into the water (whose icy edges she'd broken earlier), and eventually much of it went down her gullet. She bobs her head to work things down into the lower part of her neck, and I suppose her gizzard goes to work on them there.

Chapter Six
from A BOX OF MATCHES

Good morning, it's 6:08 a.m.—late. When I got up and stood on the landing at the top of the stairs I could see three light effects. One was the white spreadsheet of the moonlight on the floor, and one was more moonlight barred with long banister shadows on the floor downstairs, and one was the hint of pale yellow and blue of dawn arriving beyond the trees. Or maybe it was the glow of the convenience store in the next town. I got up late because I stayed up late working on that thief of time, a website. Nothing so completely sucks an evening away as fiddling with the layout of a website. By the time I was in bed reading "The Men That Don't Fit In" by Robert Service, Claire was asleep in her blue fleece bathrobe and it was eleven o'clock.

But now I'm up and little flames are growing like sedums from the cracks in today's log wall, and I still have a little while before I have to drive Phoebe to school. Every morning the coffee makes me blow my nose, and then I toss the nose-wad into the fire, and it's gone. The fire is like a cheerful dog that waits by the table as you feed it life-scraps.

Our bedroom was still quite dark when I got up. I felt for my glasses on the bedside table in that tender way one uses for glasses, as if one's fingers are antennae, so as not to get smears on them. The smear of a fingerprint makes it impossible to concentrate on anything; it's much worse than the round blur in your vision made by a speck of dust. The glasses made a little clacking sound as I sat up and put them on—oh yeah, baby. The nice thing about putting on your glasses in the dark is that you know you could see better if it were light, but since it is dark the glasses make no difference at all.

My hand seemed to know just where my glasses would be, and this reminded me of something that I noticed about five years ago in a hotel bathroom. I wish I'd taken photographs of all the hotel rooms I've been in. Some of them stay in my head for a while, and some disappear immediately—those many shades of pinky beige. I remember well two of the hotel rooms that Claire and I stayed in on our honeymoon—one a fancy one, and one in an unprosperous little town. There was a bathroom behind an accordion wall in that one.

Claire has just come to say good morning. She said that she could tell that I hadn't been up for too long today because of the newer smell of the coffee. She has a good sense of smell. In college there were coed bathrooms; one time she knew that it was I who had surreptitiously peed in the shower stall. Right now she's unhappy that the last American manufacturer of a certain kind of wooden spoon has gone out of business. She saw a woman on the news saying, "This was my life. My grandmother made spoons, my mother made spoons, and now it's finished." Claire likes old people—not just relations, but old people in general. She's become friends with the catty woman down the street, and she is used to the smell of oxygen from oxygen tanks. I'm glad she likes old people because it means that when I get old she will be less likely to be disgusted with me.

I've known Claire for—let me figure it out—twenty-three of my forty-four years. More than half my life I've loved her. Think of that. We met on the stairs of a dormitory; I was carrying my bicycle down and she and her roommate were walking upstairs carrying bags of new textbooks. We lived on Third North, the third floor on the north side, a hall of extremely young boys and girls (so they seem to be now) who, because we all shared a large bathroom, quickly became chummy. Claire and her roommate gave cocktail parties every Tuesday at 4:30, using the floor's ironing board as a bar. I walked out in the snow with them to buy the liquor: I was twenty-one, and Pennsylvania had one of those tiresome laws.

When Claire was a little drunk, she would rock slowly to reggae and her lips would get cold. Her mouth, however, was warm and her teeth sharp. I cultivated a rakishly nutty air: I discovered a fine prewar toilet on the curb and carried it into my room, propping the two-volume *Oxford English Dictionary* inside. But Claire had a thing for a very handsome sandy-haired boy named William. Many had crushes on William because he was gentle and aloof and had an appealing way of clearing his throat before he spoke. Rumor had it that his penis was unusually attractive, but I never saw it. William's father was a famous surgeon, and one day William borrowed some thread and showed us how to tie the knots that famous surgeons use on wounds. He never drank. When, maliciously, I tried to slip a little gin in his tonic, he sipped and handed the glass back to me with a reproachful look. I still feel guilty.

Claire had a thing for gentle William, as I say—and then one evening, after one of the ironing-board cocktail parties, she asked me out on a date with her to walk to the cash machine. I said that a walk to the cash machine would be very nice. In those days she wore a thrift-store cashmere coat and soft Italian sweaters and, though her mother pleaded with her, no bra. And her lips were soft, too—much softer and somehow more intelligent than others I'd kissed, and though I hadn't kissed that many lips I'd kissed some.

I went with her to the dentist when she had her wisdom teeth out. Afterward she slept curled for a long time, a small beautiful person; there on her desk in a glass of water were the two enormous teeth. They were like the femurs of bron-tosauri. How those giant teeth could have fit into her head I don't know.

So this morning when I reached for my glasses, I remembered noticing in a hotel how my hand had gotten better at knowing just where the soap was in an alien shower. My lower mind would hold in its memory a three-dimensional plan of the shower that included the possible perches for the soap: the ledge, the indented built-in soap tray, the near corner, the far corner. I would wash my face, then put the soap down somewhere without thinking about it, then shampoo; and then, still blind from the shampoo, I'd want to

wash my lower-down areas, and even though I'd been turning around and around in the shower, I was able to use the
north star of the angle of the shower-flow to orient myself,
so that without looking I could bend and find the bar of
soap under my fingers, often without any groping.

Chapter Seven
from A BOX OF MATCHES

Good morning, it's 4:19 a.m., and I can't get over how bright the moon is here. We've lived in Oldfield for over three years now and the brightness of the moon and stars is one of the most amazing things about the place. Even when there's a big chunk taken out of it, as there is now, the moon's light is powerful enough that you can sense, looking out the window, what direction it's coming from. When you look anglingly up, there's this thing high in the sky that you almost have to squint at. The small, high-up moons seem to be the brightest ones.

I fall asleep a little after ten reading a software manual, and now I'm up and waiting for the train whistle. The fire today is made partly of half-charred loggage from yesterday, but mostly from thin apple branches that I sawed up when I got home from work. I tried the ax first and had a heck of a time. But a handsaw will slide right through with wondrous ease, sprinkling handfuls of sawdust out of either side of the cut, like—like I can't think what—like a sower sowing seeds, perhaps. Anyway the fire took to burning so readily that I've had to move my chair back a little so that my legs aren't in pain through the flannel.

The thing that is so great about sitting here in the early morning is that it doesn't matter what I did all yesterday: my mind only connects with fire-thoughts. I have an apple to eat if I want to eat it—picked in the fall and refrigerated in a state of semi-permanent crispness.

The whole dropping-of-the-leaves thing and the coming of winter is one of those gradual processes that becomes harder to believe each year it happens. All those leaves were up there firmly attached to the trees, and they're gone. Now, incredibly, there are *no leaves on the trees.* And not only that, but it's becoming impossible to conceive that there ever would have been leaves on the trees. It's like death, which is also becoming harder and harder for me to understand. How could someone you know and remember so well be dead? My grandmother, for instance. I can't believe that she is dead. I don't mean that I believe in a hereafterly world, I don't. But it does seem puzzling to me that she is now not living.

This year there was a particular moment of leaf-falling that I hadn't encountered before. I went outside at sunrise to feed the duck—this was sometime in October. There was ice in her water when she jumped in: hard pieces of something that she thought might be good to eat but weren't particularly when she tumbled and smacked them around with her beak. While I was waiting for my daughter Phoebe to come out, I began scraping off the thin ice layer on the windshield using my AAA card, and then I heard a leafy rustling a few hundred years away. I looked in the direction of the sound, expecting to see a coon cat or a fox. What I saw, instead, was a middle-sized, yellow-leafed sugar maple tree. It was behaving oddly: all of its leaves were dropping off at the same time. It wasn't the wind—there was no wind. I stood there for a while, watching the tree denude itself at this unusual pace, and I came up with a theory to explain the simultaneity of the unleaving. The tree was not as tall as some of the other trees—that's the first thing. And it was the first night-freeze of the year. So we can imagine all the twigs of the tree coated with the same thin but tenacious coat of ice that I was encountering on the windshield. Now the sun had risen enough to clear the dense hummock of forest across the creek, and thus sunlight was striking and warming the leaves on this particular tree for the first time since they'd frozen. The night-ice had sheathed the skin, holding the leaf in place, but the freeze had also caused the final rupture in the parenchymatous cells that attached the leaf-stem to its twig: as soon as the ice melted, the leaf fell. I had some confirmation of my theory when I noticed that the leaves on the sun-ward side of the tree were mainly the ones that were falling.

My son, who is eight, had a plan for the leaves this year. He filled six large kraft-paper bags with them, and saved them in the barn, so that when my brother and sister-in-law came to visit with their children he could make an enormous pile. His plan worked, which is not true of all his plans. The pile was big and the leaves were dry, not soggy, and my sister-in-law and I took lots of pictures of smiling children leaping around piles of leaves and flinging them in the air, and I had that moment of slight fear when I knew the future. I knew that we would remember this moment better than other perhaps worthier or more representative moments because we were taking pictures of it. The duck hovered near the rake, hoping that we would get down to a slimy underlayer where the worms lived. But there wasn't one.

I found out yesterday that one of the town elders has died. He sounded perfectly fine over the phone when I talked to him in November—gravelly-voiced but fine. When I was taking out the garbage yesterday, walking up the ramp that leads into the barn, I suddenly imagined this aged man turning from a living human being to skull and bones—and I was amazed in the same way that I'm amazed when the leaves fall and we're left with skeletal trees every year. Really I'm glad my grandparents were cremated. I don't like the idea that their skulls would be around somewhere. Better and more dignified for them to be completely parceled out.

Good morning, it's 4:50 a.m.—I just took such a deep bite of red apple that it pushed my lower lip all the way down to where the lip joins up with the chin. There is a clonk point there, and a good apple can do that, push your lower lip down to its clonk point. Sometimes you think for a moment that you're going to get stuck in the apple because you can't bite down any farther. But all you have to do is push the apple a little to the left—or pull it to the right—and let the half-bitten chunk break off in your mouth. If you do it slowly, it sounds like a tree falling in the forest. Then start chewing.

Phoebe said something yesterday on the way to school that I thought was very true. While I was finishing feeding the duck, she came out in her perfectly ironed blue jeans, carrying a piece of toast in her mittens and crouching like a Sherpa beneath the load of her backpack. She's fourteen. We both got in the car, and I turned the heater on full. It roared and hurled out a blast of icy air. Phoebe held a mitten over her mouth and nose and said, "It's cold, Dad, it's cold." I said, "You're not kidding it's cold—it's *really* cold."

As I took hold of the steering wheel, I made an exaggeratedly convulsive noise of frozenness, and Phoebe looked over and saw that I was hatless. Then she noticed that my hat—a tweed hat with a silk inner band—was stuffed down near the hand brake. It had been in the car all night, cooling down. She reached for it, and in that abrupt way that people have when they're trying to conserve warmth, she held it out to me. "Put this on," she said.

The thick tweed looked tempting, but I knew better and I said, "If I put this on I'm going to freeze."

She took the hat back from me and held it over the heater vents for a few seconds. "Try it now," she said.

The heater, as it turned out, had not warmed the hat to any perceptible degree: the silk inner band was a ring of ice and my head recoiled at the chill. I said: "Yow, yes, that's going to be better."

"You've got to get cold to get warm," Phoebe said.

Now that is the truth. That is so true about so many things. You learn it first with sheets and blankets: that the initial touch of the smooth sheets will send you shivering, but their warming works fast, and you must experience the discomfort to find the later contentment. It's true with money and love, too. You've got to save to have something to spend. Think of how hard it is to ask out a person you like. In my case, Claire asked me to go on a date to the cash machine, so I didn't actually have to ask her. Still, her lips were cold, but her tongue was warm.

By the time I dropped Phoebe off and gave her a dollar for a snack, my hat was as comfortably situated on my head as if it had hung on the coat tree all night.

Henry was building a Mars city when I got home from work. He went upstairs and came out of his room with an enormous Rubbermaid storage container full of Legos. It seemed bigger than he could handle. Each Lego piece is as light as a raisin, but they become heavy in the aggregate.

"Do you need some help with that?" I asked him.

"No, thanks, I think I can do it," said Henry.

"That's certainly a lot of Legos," I said.

"Dad, you should see how I get it up the stairs. It takes me about an hour." He stepped down each step very slowly, his heels treading on the edges of his too-long sweatpants. "Sometimes I get in hard situations where I'm balanced on one toe. It's not very pleasant."

I've turned the top half-log over—it looks like a glowing side of beef now.

VINTAGE BOOKS BY NICHOLSON BAKER

A Box of Matches

Nicholson Baker explores the thoughts of a man named Emmett who wakes every day before dawn to try and figure out what life is about.
Fiction/0-375-70603-8

Double Fold

With meticulous detective work and Baker's well-known explanatory power, *Double Fold* reveals a secret history of the destruction of hundreds of thousands of historic newspapers. *Double Fold* is a persuasive and often devastating look at the American library system.
Nonfiction/0-375-72621-7

The Everlasting Story of Nory

Our supreme fabulist of the ordinary now offers an enchanting idiosyncratic portrait of nine-year-old Nory Winslow. In this precocious child he gives us a heroine as canny and as whimsical as Lewis Carroll's Alice and evokes childhood in all its luminous weirdness.
Fiction/Literature/0-679-76375-9

The Fermata

Outrageously arousing, acrobatically stylish, *The Fermata* may be the most successful fusion of literature and eros since Ovid and Boccaccio.

Fiction/0-679-75933-6

The Mezzanine

Startlingly inventive and filled with offbeat wit, this wondrous novel turns a ride up the escalator of an office building into a dazzling meditation on our most familiar relations with objects and one another.

Fiction/0-679-72576-8

Room Temperature

Nicholson Baker transforms a young father's feeding-time reverie into a dazzling catalog of the minutiae of domestic love.

Fiction/0-679-73440-6

The Size of Thoughts

In this irresistible first collection of essays Nicholson Baker measures the precise circumference of thoughts. The result is a provocative and often hilarious celebration of the neglected aspects of our experience, by a writer of stunning intelligence and inimitable charm.

Nonfiction/essays/0-679-77624-9

U and I

Baker constructs a splendid edifice that is at once a tribute to John Updike and a disarmingly, often hilariously frank self-examination—a work that lays bare both the pettiest and the most exalted transactions between writers and their readers.

Literature/Nonfiction/0-679-73575-5

Vox

Vox remaps the territory of sex—sex solitary and telephonic, lyrical and profane, comfortable and dangerous. It is an erotic classic that places Nicholson Baker firmly in the first rank of major American writers.

Fiction/0-679-74211-5

Coming in Summer 2005

Checkpoint

Meet Jay.
Meet Ben.
Jay has summoned his old friend Ben to a hotel room not far from the nation's capitol. During the course of an afternoon, they will share a delicious lunch and will crack open a bottle of wine from the hotel minibar. They will chat about everything from Ben's new camera to Iraq to the unfortunate fate of a particular free-range chicken. And Jay will explain to Ben exactly why and how he is planning to commit a murder that will change the course of history.

Fiction/1-4000-7985-3

VINTAGE **READERS**

Authors available in this series

Martin Amis

Nicholson Baker

James Baldwin

A. S. Byatt

Willa Cather

Sandra Cisneros

Joan Didion

Richard Ford

Langston Hughes

Barry Lopez

V. S. Naipaul

Alice Munro

Haruki Murakami

Vladimir Nabokov

Michael Ondaatje

Oliver Sacks

Representing a wide spectrum of some of our most significant modern and contemporary authors, the Vintage Readers offer an attractive, accessible selection of writing that matters.